THE THREE HARES

BOOK 2

THE GOLD MONKEY KEY

THE THREE HARES

BOOK 2
THE GOLD MONKEY KEY

BY SCOTT LAUDER
AND DAVID ROSS

NEEM TREE
PRESS

Published by Neem Tree Press Limited 2021

Neem Tree Press Limited
95A Ridgmount Gardens, London, WC1E 7AZ
info@neemtreepress.com

Copyright © Scott Lauder and David Ross, 2021
A catalogue record for this book is available from the British Library

ISBN 978-1-911107-07-1 Paperback
ISBN 978-1-911107-12-5 Ebook

Printed and bound in Great Britain
by Biddles Limited

CONTENTS

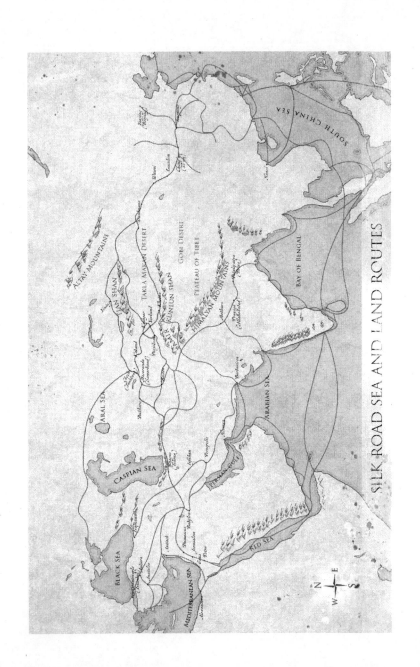

SILK ROAD SEA AND LAND ROUTES

PART 1

ATHENS, GREECE; KOWLOON AND HANGZHOU, CHINA — THE PRESENT DAY

CHAPTER 1

At the Acropolis, the winter sun fell on the citadel's ancient buildings perched on the hillside. In summer, the temperature soared beyond 35 degrees, the air was choked and the light blinding. Winter was different. The traffic eased, the air cleared, and the sun was no longer a fiery demon, Instead, it became a cheerful friend – yellowing quince, warming the bones of old Athenians and brightening unshuttered apartments.

But in a stinking room, not far from the Acropolis, the space was as dark as a tomb.

Chan sniffed the air in Pythias's apartment. It smelled as if something once alive had long ago decomposed in a forgotten corner. Chan had come to Athens in the hope that Pythias could help him. Pythias, the great oracle – knower of secrets, teller of fortunes, and, Chan hoped, furnisher of miracles. After crossing and re-crossing continents in his search for someone who could tell him where the Jade Dragonball was, Chan needed a miracle, and Pythias, in this festering apartment, was his last hope.

Chan waited for his eyes to adjust to the darkness. Although a shaft of light was pushing through a gap in the heavy curtains, it was too narrow to fully illuminate the cluttered room. Slowly, Chan began to see books stacked on tables and chairs. They rose in musty columns, like Hunan's stone pillars. At any other time, Chan would have loved to rummage through the stacks and add to his vast library, but he had other priorities today. Chan and his men wove their way past them. Through the gloom, he also caught sight of a long mirror, its gold frame luminous in the half-light. In its antique glass, he saw himself: a white silk cravat and an elegant dark blue suit, a face craggy with drooping cheeks; puffed and wrinkled eyes; thin, grey hair. His appearance surprised people. He knew that. It was the result of a rare genetic condition. The ageing process had gone into hyperdrive the moment he was born. He was just seventeen years old, but he looked like an old man of seventy.

The darkness was annoying him. Sunlight was not much use to a blind man like Pythias, but Chan had eyes and could use them! But as he reached to open the curtain, a voice ordered him not to touch it. Chan smiled. Very well. He moved forward again when there was a loud crash behind him. One of his men had knocked over a tower of books. 'Leave it,' Chan ordered.

A few more turns and he found himself standing beside a low wooden trestle table. Behind it was an immense couch. The flickering flame of a single candle illuminated a mountain of a man on it, propped up by pillows. The long, unkempt hair shrouding his face was as white as the robe that lay around him. Pythias the Greek. Whispers of the thoughts of his men whirled around and through Chan but Pythias's mind was completely still, or impenetrable.

'Bring the bird,' Pythias ordered, his voice raspy, as though his throat were filled with dust.

Chan nodded and gestured to An Ho, his personal bodyguard. In An Ho's meaty hand was a bamboo birdcage covered by a red cotton cloth. Not a word was said as he passed it to Chan, who passed it to Pythias.

From under the cloth came a sharp squawk and a rustling of feathers.

Pythias stretched out his fingers, unerringly finding the handle on the cage. 'It is a mysterious thing, that which you ask,' he said. 'Yet it shall be a mystery no longer.'

The room was silent but for the sounds coming from the cage. There was a shuffling behind Chan and his men. The attendant who had opened the front door had returned and was carrying a shallow cauldron, which he set upon a tripod on the table in front of Pythias. Inside the cauldron, a pile of wood lay upon pages ripped from a book. The attendant retreated, bowing as he went.

'We will put your question to the bird and await its answer,' Pythias said, and he reached out and whisked the cloth off the cage. Inside it, a bird hopped from perch to perch nervously. Pythias pulled a box of matches off the side table, removed a match and struck it. In the feeble light, Chan made out Pythias's eyes. Though the eyelids were closed, his eyeballs, rolling below the loose skin, darted left and right.

'Let us begin,' Pythias said, and tossed the match into the cauldron. The fire spread through the sticks inside; thick smoke rose, carrying with it a sickly sweet odour. He waved his hand through the air slowly, brushing the smoke towards the birdcage.

The bird had bright white markings around its eyes that looked painted against its russet and grey feathers. Its green eyes glittered in the fire's light. Chan's men had done as Pythias had asked and brought a *hwamei* – a spectacled thrush. The colourful bird fluttered its wings and suddenly began hopping around energetically as the smoke engulfed it.

'Ask your question,' Pythias said. 'The bird's song will tell me the future.'

Chan's heart raced in anticipation. A series of images spun through his mind like a movie that had been sped up: places he had gone, people he had met – monks, Taoist priests, shamans... How many different paths he had followed, how many dead ends! Was he at last close to finding the answers he sought? 'Where is the Jade Dragonball?' he asked, his voice level, hiding the excitement that dared to bubble up inside him.

For a moment, the bird stopped and tilted its head as if listening. It hopped onto the opposite perch, stopped again. Chan stared at it, waiting for its yellow beak to open. A silence fell that threatened never to end.

Finally, Pythias reached out and tapped the cage with a finger.

Nothing happened.

He hit the top of the cage with his fist and waited again.

Still nothing.

Sighing deeply, he flipped open the latch of the cage. The hwamei, startled, beat its wings frantically, crashing into the bars. Pythias waited for a moment with his hand on the floor of the cage, then struck, grabbing the hwamei in his fist. The bird struggled briefly before falling quiet.

Chan looked into its spectacled eyes. *It knows but refuses to tell*, he thought. *All of nature has been called upon to guard the secret.*

Pythias removed the hwamei from the cage and held it above the embers of the fire. With one smooth movement, he snapped its neck. 'Song is not all that can be interpreted – smoke does equally well,' he said, tossing the bird on the burning embers.

CHAPTER 2

The hwamei smouldered for a few moments before catching fire. Smoke curled up in thin wisps from its body, gathering in the air above the tripod in a small cloud. The stench of burning flesh and feathers wafted through the dark room.

'Ask your question again, this time with your mind alone,' Pythias said. 'Let it fill your mind as water fills a submerged cup.'

Chan focused his attention on the smoke spreading in front of him so that the surrounding room and everything inside it faded and disappeared.

As he watched, the wisps of smoke wove themselves together, drawing a tapestry in the air. A circular shape emerged, a shape that at first looked like the one that had haunted his dreams these many years. He grew tense. More strands of smoke adhered, sliding and binding with the image that hung before him. Colours flared. The parts of the circle began to come together, rotating – but what was this? The smoke shifted… Was this a joke? Why was he seeing *rabbits*? Anger overtook him so quickly for a moment he struggled to control his breathing. *Perhaps the Greek's neck will break as easily as the bird's*, he thought.

The image lasted for a moment as the smoke continued to swirl.

'What do you see?' Pythias asked, tilting his head to one side as if he were listening to the smoke. 'Tell me.'

Chan opened his mouth to answer as a new shape emerged, its tail flicking from side to side, its scales gleaming. 'A… a fish,' he said, watching in amazement as the swirling mass in front of him shimmered and faded. A third image was forming. Chan gasped and reached out a hand. It passed straight through what was now before him: the shimmering Jade Dragonball, the dragons on its surface writhing, snapping and roaring mutely. 'Yes… Yes!' Chan cried, but even as the words were leaving his lips, the image was growing greyer, its colours seeping away. He made one more lunge, one more futile attempt to grasp the ball, but it was no longer there. Then, to his surprise, the smoke swirled again, twisting and contorting like a tiny whirlwind. A fourth object, much smaller than its real-life counterpart, spun into existence – its arms, legs and torso a patchwork collection of multi-coloured shiny squares. This was something Chan recognised, something he knew he would need for Project Tian Shan. A moment later, it too was gone, and the air between Chan and the Greek was empty once again.

'I saw four things,' Chan said, his voice hoarse with pleasure. 'Two objects I understood; two I did not.'

'Describe those you did not understand,' Pythias said.

Chan recounted his two puzzling visions: the rabbits that appeared to chase one another in a circle, and the fish. Pythias, his hands clasped in front of his face, was silent for a long time after Chan had finished.

One of Chan's goons, growing impatient, whispered in Chan's ear. 'You sure we can trust him, boss?'

Chan nodded calmly at the man before turning back to the oracle. The room was silent once again except for the cracking of the hwamei's bones as they splintered in the flames.

'Yes, I understand now,' Pythias said. 'You will forgive the wait. I have seen a place that lies far beyond time.'

'And what have you learned?' Chan asked, leaning forward.

'What you seek has been caught in the net of your desire.' The old man gave a wheezing laugh.

Chan leaned back. 'Speak plainly, old man,' he snapped. 'I want the Jade Dragonball. Where is it?' He breathed deeply, fighting to regain his composure.

Pythias seemed unworried by his guest's change in mood. 'The wind is strongest at the summit. As the time nears, know you shall not go unopposed. Forces are being summoned from afar. They will join and three will become one.'

The wrinkled skin around Chan's mouth curled back, the snarl revealing the gleaming-white veneers hiding his discoloured teeth. 'No one can match my resources, so let *me* worry about any opposition. Again, I ask: where? Where is the Dragonball?'

Pythias's voice was steady. 'The smoke talks but does not spell.'

Chan's frustration ignited his anger. The old man had not given him the answers he sought... but what if his powers of prophesy rose and fell? What if someone else came looking for the Dragonball and Pythias was somehow able to delve deeper into the world beyond?

Chan rubbed his cheek with his hand. So, should he take the old fool with him? Pythias, chuckling to himself, bulbous rolls of fat beneath his chin wobbling as he enjoyed a joke that only he had heard, seemed to feel Chan's gaze on him. He stopped laughing and peered back, a quizzical look on his enormous, round face.

The old man clearly had *some* ability: after all, he had conjured two objects that made sense. But rabbits? Fish? Such nonsense!

And what about the size of him? How would he get such an enormous... *creature* off its couch, out the door and into a car, never mind on an aircraft? Pythias suddenly went still. No. There was a far simpler solution. Chan rose stiffly.

A lifetime of telling fortunes had hardened the oracle to the point where he no longer flinched. 'What you seek shall be yours. But there is always a cost. It may be wiser to let things be.'

Chan stared at the blind man and thought of the years of searching that had led him here. Was Pythias seriously suggesting he abandon his quest? He snapped his fingers at his men. 'Pay him,' Chan said, addressing An Ho and pointing to the old man. After a long moment he added, 'And then kill him.'

CHAPTER 3

—

Chan was jet-lagged and aching after his trip to Athens: his body felt like a collection of dirty clothes left in a spin drier. Grimacing, he rose to his feet and straightened his back. Then, using his cane for support, he paced to the glass that protruded like a giant eye into the mist-streaked air high above the harbour. Far below, ocean-going tankers and bulk carriers crawled across the bays of northern Hong Kong – Hung Hom, Tsau Wan, To Kwa Wan – no bigger than ants.

Even though Chan was looking out of the window of the most luxurious penthouse in all of Kowloon, he felt trapped in a gold cage. The spacious room – lined with books, decorated with fine silk hangings, richly polished wood and chrome –suffocated him.

He picked up *The Business*, Hong Kong's most popular business newspaper. As usual, news about Bai Lu wasn't far from the front page.

Today there was further good news for the conglomerate Bai Lu as one of Asia's biggest private equity firms, Redwood Blaze, announced it had taken an additional 1.5% stake in the company, bringing its total holding to 3.2%. News of the investment by Redwood Blaze saw shares in Bai Lu rise by over 17%, which will be welcome news for the Hong Kong-based firm after a series of scandals saw three of its top scientists arrested on charges of insider trading and its share price plummet. Shares of Bai Lu, up 6.7% overall this year, closed at an all-time high of $14.74, a price that represents a market capitalisation value for Bai Lu of $7.33 bn.

Chan gave a dry chuckle. The arrests had been a setback. But the recent fall in Bai Lu's share price hadn't worried him: he was sure that what went down would also come up again. And looking at Bai Lu's share price now, a record high, he had been correct to stay calm and optimistic. However, what did concern him was the loss of expertise. He would have to recruit others: the success of Bai Lu – and more importantly Project Tian Shan – depended on it.

According to *The Business* and anyone else who knew anything about biogenetics, Lin Dan was the most respected, most accomplished, researcher in China. Lin Dan, Chan reflected, was like the Jade Dragonball: infuriatingly out of reach. Not that Chan hadn't tried to recruit him. He had used his subordinates in Shanghai to speak to Lin Dan many times, but all their efforts to persuade him had failed. Perhaps the prospect of a 200% pay rise had not been enough? Perhaps he was unwilling to leave Shanghai, where his wife and daughter lived and where his laboratory was situated, for Chan's project in Xi'an? Chan had offered Lin Dan many carrots, but if that approach didn't bear fruit soon, or if the Jade Dragonball were found, he would have to change his tactics…

Chan tossed the newspaper away, rubbed his dry, puffy eyes and slid open the glass door to the balcony. A brisk wind greeted him, smarting his face and ruffling his hair. He didn't mind. Shuffling across the balcony's expansive decking, he reached the aluminium rail and clasped it. The whole of the peninsula lay before him: to the west, Stonecutter's Island; to the north, the beautiful Lei Yue Mun strait and the tiny white-sailed boats skipping along it. Below, the city of Kowloon rumbled, vibrant with life. He thought of how much of the city, with all its gangs and hustlers, its back rooms and alleys, was in his control… and how it wasn't enough, wasn't what he was truly seeking. He had just turned seventeen, yet his years of searching felt like fifty.

He stared out, trying to gauge the best way to proceed. So many possible roads. So many choices… Could Pythias have been right, that he should let things be? A flutter of wings disturbed his thoughts.

Perched upon the balcony rail was a small bird with a yellow beak and white rings around its eyes. Chan blinked to make sure it was still there when he opened his eyes. It sat there still – a hwamei.

Chan stared at the bird curiously. Had the bird come back from the dead to tell him after all?

The thrush tilted its head and Chan half expected it to speak. Instead, it opened its beak and sang – a song that sounded like laughter, mocking him. Chan lunged at the bird, but it hopped along the rail, just beyond his reach. A wave of frustration lashed through him, fuelled by years of hunting for some clue, any clue, that gave him direction, something that would enable him to proceed with his plan. Chan grasped the gold pen protruding from his pocket and hurled it at the thrush. It missed, twinkled briefly in the sunlight, and tumbled to the streets below.

The bird flapped its wings and, as suddenly as it had appeared, vanished.

Chan, breathing hard, looked once more up at the sky, watching the clouds, admiring their infinite reach; their limitless ability to regenerate. Today, they were soft, pearl-white, drifting. But in a storm, they darkened, they towered, they flashed: sending down rain that could drown cities and lightning bolts that snaked from the heavens and struck the earth with awesome, terrifying power. Clouds were a force of nature. And the forces of nature – their gentleness and murderous strength – were a mirror of himself.

Closing the balcony door, he sunk into the thickly cushioned chair behind his desk and closed his eyes. The squawking of the hwamei still rang in his ears. The sound tugged his memory, taking him back to Pythias's darkened room. He recalled the oracle's face lit from underneath by the glow of the brazier; again – for what must have been the thousandth time – he stared as the strands of smoke weaved and grew solid, form dragons that crawled on the jade ball's gleaming surface; and once again, he reached out to the image, grasping unsuccessfully for the ball… Despite hours of frustrated contemplation, two of the visions remained mystifying: the rabbits and the fish.

There was a knock at the door. 'Come,' Chan cried, irritated.

It opened and a man was pushed roughly into the room, so hard he stumbled on the plush cream carpet and landed in a heap in front of Chan's desk. An Ho, pausing for a moment at the threshold to lower his stubbled head in a bow, followed the man in and yanked him to his knees. The terror in the man's eyes turned to amazement at the luxuriousness of the office he now found himself in. An Ho, his hand still gripping the man's suit collar and holding it high above the man's head, gave the man a shake.

'Kwan here says he has run into some difficulties, Mr Chan. I thought it best that he speak with you.'

Chan's anger at being disturbed, at having to retake the reins again, of having to make, for the millionth time, another of the decisions that would steer his sprawling empire, flashed at An Ho. Sometimes he felt so worn, so ready just to… step back, let it all go, be a nobody, a nothing. But he knew that could never happen: he was either the leader, or he was dead. No presumptive successor would risk allowing him to retire: he knew too much and would be a potential rallying point for any disaffected gang members. But more importantly – far, far more importantly – he knew himself. His desires and ambitions gripped him, vice like, and would always demand he kept going.

He glanced at Kwan. Kwan was the leader of a gang of three hundred men in the south-western part of the city. He was a valuable source of revenue for Chan's syndicate. In other words, someone who needed his... guidance.

Whispering furiously, Kwan's thoughts floated through Chan's head. To Chan, his mind was a great tree filled with leaves and the thoughts of others were breezes that often skirted its bough, but occasionally shook its leaves, setting in motion a quivering, rippling song that became vowels, consonants, words. And the song he heard now made him angry. Kwan had been gambling. He'd tried to recover his losses and thrown away even more money. He had sold his car, but the money in his pocket from its sale was only a quarter of the amount due. Chan scoffed silently. The most powerful thought in Kwan's stupid head? It seemed his bladder would not be able to withstand much more stress...

'Ah, yes, Mr Kwan. I had not heard from you or your men in many days.' He nodded to An Ho, who released Kwan's collar. 'Please forgive An Ho – his other responsibilities have made him quite indelicate.'

The tough face Kwan presented to his men, his constant sneer and glare, was gone. His eyes darted around the room, avoiding the hard look Chan was giving him. His crumpled black suit seemed too large, especially as he tried to hide inside it.

Chan reached across his desk and opened a small gold box. 'As you know, for our protection of your business interests, we expect you to uphold your end of the deal, Mr Kwan.' From the box, Chan removed a slice of mooncake, exquisitely made by his personal chef. Popping it in his mouth, he stood a moment, silently enjoying the cake's soft red-bean filling before continuing. 'We ask little, yet even that seems too much. You are two months behind on your payments, Mr Kwan. Two months is more than I believe reasonable, is it not?' Chan didn't wait for an answer. 'I am sure you know of your predecessor. A Mr... ah, what was it... Sung? Shang? Alas, I have forgotten. Perhaps you have forgotten as well. Such a pity about his accidental death.'

Kwan, a trickle of sweat rolling down the side of his face, opened his mouth to offer his excuse. He knew what he said would determine whether or not he lived. Before he could speak, though, there was a loud knock at the door.

Chan looked up. 'Not now,' he said, expecting whoever it was to go away. But to the surprise of all present, the door opened. An Ho reached for the gun in his shoulder holster, but stopped when he saw it was Yang, another top-ranking bodyguard. Whereas An Ho was all muscle, Yang was small and slender. Just as dangerous as An Ho, Yang was a dagger whereas An Ho was an axe. Taking no notice of Kwan sprawled at An Ho's feet, Yang entered and bowed deeply, bobbing up and down as he approached Chan, his floppy hair falling over his eyes. 'Very important news, boss. Very, very important.' Yang cupped a hand and whispered in Chan's ear.

For a moment, Chan stood, too astounded to move, the sounds pouring into his ears too sweet to be real. He stared at Yang. Yang was serious. 'It has been found,' he said.

As Yang continued, describing the location – Shengsi, a small group of islands in southern China – Chan listened intently. How long had this day taken to arrive? How much he had to do now that it had come! He barked some orders at Yang, who bowed and galloped out of the room. Pitiful snivelling brought his mind back to the terrified man cowering in front of him.

'The world is full of surprises, Mr Kwan. You might say this is your lucky day – lucky because it will not likely be your last.' The smile remained even as he spoke. 'You will be given another

chance. You will bring us the money we are due – within one week.'
Chan waved his hand in the air, signalling that the meeting was
over. Kwan was dragged to his feet once more. He even tried to bow
as An Ho pulled him towards the door. A moment later, he and An
Ho were gone.

Chan's heart was hammering. Shakily, he sat and took hold of
the photograph on the table. He looked at his mother. The yellow
of her dress, the yellow of the flower in her hair were pale, almost
white. She had died when Chan was only seven years old. They
had both travelled to her village with Grandfather Wei to meet
her parents and her village friends after a long time. She never
returned.

Some said it was the water from the village well, that it had
become poisoned, deadly. One minute the villagers were strong and
healthy; the next they were coughing up blood, dropping to their
knees, breathing their last, tortured breath on the dusty ground. It
was said a local warlord had poisoned the well – an act of brutality
in retaliation for some unintended insult. Others believed it was a
demon's work. No one knew for sure. In the end, half the village
had died. His mother and her parents had been amongst the first.
But Grandfather Wei, newly arrived after attending a funeral in a
neighbouring village, had not drunk from the well. Instead, he had
reacted quickly, picking up and gently placing the feverish little
Chan in his cart, and left, travelling to Hangzhou where his son –
Chan's father – lived, never to return to the village. Grandfather Wei
had nursed little Chan back to health.

Chan thought he could still remember his mother's delicate
smell, the sound of her soft voice, her laughter as they played
hide and seek around their home. But perhaps it was all in his
imagination? All he knew was when he recalled his mother, his heart
softened a little.

Gently, Chan placed the photograph down. How he wished his father were alive to see him take what was now within his grasp. How jealous – *how infuriated* – he would be! No accomplishment, feat or victory – his father's or anyone else's – could hope to match what would soon be his.

CHAPTER 4

—

Chan stared down from the helicopter at the green-grey water, a flickering blanket stretching to the horizon.

He was near Hangzhou in Zhejiang province. Though Bai Lu had its main office in Dunhuang, Hangzhou had, many years ago, been the seat of his father's power. It was the place his father had first murdered a man – a competitor now buried in the foundations of an office block, one of the hundreds his father's construction companies had built. His father had made Bai Lu a powerful, multi-billion-dollar company, but the company stretched all the way back to the Northern Song Dynasty.

It was an ancestor, Shan Tuo, who had started a criminal gang called Bai Lu and come up with its motto: *Establish the Hegemon*. Not that Chan had any great love for Shan Tuo – he was the ancestor whose debilitating genetic condition had been passed down through the generations to him. But he did love Shan Tuo's brother, Shan Wu… Chan chuckled. How absurd it was: after travelling to every corner of the globe, it was here, in the watery depths surrounding Hangzhou, that his dream of finding the Dragonball had once more come alive.

In the distance, dotting the sea, were the Shengsi Islands. The helicopter stuck to the coastline, its insect-like shadow cast on the tree-topped mountains that crowded the shore. They banked around an outcropping cliff-face and cut back inland, out over a field of millet, out towards a clearing with seven cars parked around the periphery. One, parked a bit further out, was a black limo with tinted windows, sunlight glinting off its polished surface. A man standing beside it bowed as the helicopter drew near, keeping his head down as the copter hovered above the centre of the clearing, insensitive to the pillows of dust it kicked up as it landed.

An Ho was the first to step out of the copter. A large man, his broad frame filled the doorway of the cabin as he jumped down lightly. He ducked his head and walked out to the waiting cars, pistol in hand. In front of each car stood a head of the local chapter of Chan's syndicate. Once An Ho had determined that it was safe, he signalled to Chan, who slowly stepped down from the copter, brushed the dust off his shoulders and straightened his grey suit.

Chan waited for the rotors to stop before addressing the men surrounding him, many of whom were twenty, even thirty years older than him. Nevertheless, they stood at attention, even as the sun shone brightly on their faces. Chan raised his voice so all would hear. 'I would like to thank you for meeting me here today.'

The men around the circle greeted him formally, each placing his left fist in his right hand and bowing from the waist, as did each of their drivers, who stood on the circle's outer side. They respectfully held this position for a long moment before coming back to attention. A strong breeze blew across the fields, carrying the salty tang of the sea.

Chan looked around the circle at each of the men in turn. All had been in the service of his father, had helped build the syndicate up from its base in Hangzhou, had risen to power as they gained control of more cities, more provinces. They had feared his father, who was dead a year. In that time, Chan had shown them they would be wise to fear him more.

'You have worked hard. Our profits in this region have increased. That is good. You have been loyal. And that is good, too. Such loyalty deserves rewards. Soon, a project I have in Xi'an will come to fruition. When it does, you will be part of a syndicate that will make you amongst the richest men in the world.'

A murmur of excitement and appreciation rippled around the crowd. Chan smiled. He held up his hand and there was silence again.

'But what reward does *dis*loyalty bring?' he asked, pausing, allowing the question to linger, watching the smiles fade, the anxiety on the men's tough faces grow. 'Hmm?' He cast his eyes around the circle, enjoying the sight of many lowering their heads, clearly unable to meet his gaze. 'What if,' he continued, 'a *dis*loyal servant was playing with the accounts? What if he were pretending the profits were smaller than they really were? What if he were putting *my* money in his own pocket? What reward should such a person get? Hmm?'

Unseen by most of the others standing in the circle, An Ho had quietly gone and stood behind a tall, grey-haired man whose face had gone pale and whose eyes darted from side to side. As though he felt An Ho's massive presence behind him, the man turned. He screamed, but An Ho's powerful arms wrapped themselves around the man's body, snuffing out the man's cry, pinning the man's arms to his side, and lifting him off the ground.

'In my opinion, the best the reward,' Chan said, watching as the man squirmed and wriggled like a worm on a hook, 'is a short helicopter ride over the sea.' He nodded, and An Ho began shuffling towards the helicopter, the man trapped in his arms yelling at Chan and begging for forgiveness. As everyone watched, An Ho threw the man into the arms of others who bundled the man into the helicopter. And as An Ho returned to Chan's side, the helicopter rose into the air, banked, and pointed its nose towards the open sea.

The rest of the short meeting continued without incident, but it was only when Chan's limo was out of sight that the men dared to breathe easily once again.

The limo glided through the mountain pass and rounded one last bend to reveal a small bay. Chan watched it come into view and tried to quell the anticipation bubbling within him. The beach was throbbing with activity. Long boats lined the shore, their ancient-looking wooden hulls pulled onto the sand after the day's haul. The line stretched right back to the fishermen's huts that were huddled along the base of the mountain.

As they drew closer, Chan watched the fishermen busy below – some mending the keels of their boats, others repairing nets. He imagined he could hear them talking: those with large fish boasting their catches while those who had come back empty-handed telling stories about their bad luck. Day in, day out, their whole lives lived according to the rhythms of the sea.

Little did they know that the key to immortality lay amongst them.

CHAPTER 5

The limo slid up to the docks, nosing its way through the crowd of fishermen like a shark. When it reached the dock, An Ho got out of the car, buttoned his grey suit, and opened Chan's door. Chan stepped out, wrinkling his nose at the rank smell hanging in the air. An Ho swung the door shut behind him and smoothly stepped in front, putting himself between his boss and the dirty fishermen. The braver of these had stopped gawking and were now pushing forward, their catch dangling on the end of hooks or flopping about in large nets.

'Stay back!' An Ho barked as they drew near, the threat in his voice palpable.

'Does sir care for octopus?' said an old man, holding out a large, squirming octopus in a bucket for Chan to see.

'I said back!' An Ho shouted. He gave the fisherman a shove, hard enough to send him crashing into the others watching and knocking over the bucket. The freed octopus began its crawl back towards the water.

His action had the desired effect – the rest of the people parted to make way for Chan.

'Where is he?' Chan asked An Ho.

An Ho turned to one of the fishermen. 'Get me Zhou Shi,' he said. 'Now!'

A few moments later, a young man came running towards the group still standing by the limo. Instead of the rags the fishermen wore, he was wearing a sharp, dark suit. As he ran, he held his bright red tie – silk, guessed Chan, pressing it against his chest so it would not flap around. The young man slowed and bowed. Tall and slender, he had quick, intelligent eyes and a narrow, eager face. Chan was impressed, though he did not show it. 'Zhou Shi at your service, boss.'

The other fishermen stared in mute amazement. They had been working side by side with this young man for the last two years. He had told everyone he was poor, a nobody. Yet here he was, dressed like one of the emperor's cousins and speaking to a rich old man flanked by bodyguards!

'Where is it?' Chan asked impatiently.

Zhou Shi pointed to a house near the end of the beach. 'The house belongs to Mr Yu,' he said.

Chan nodded, climbed out of the car and stood next to An Ho, who was carrying a suitcase he had taken from the trunk of the car. With Zhou Shi leading the way, they strode briskly along the beach to the hut.

As if on cue, all of the fishermen began talking amongst themselves.

'I told you it would bring good luck,' one said.

'He was only able to catch it because I make such good nets!' said another.

'No! It is only because he went where I told him!' shouted a third.

Their curiosity overcoming their pride, the men stopped arguing and looked towards Mr Yu's hut. Keeping a safe distance between themselves and the visitors, they followed to see how things would turn out. More villagers noticed the group heading towards Yu's hut and joined them.

Two children, their clothes dirty and frayed, were playing outside Yu's hut. When they saw the men in suits coming their way, both jumped to their feet and ran inside the house.

The fisherman's wife came to the door just as An Ho reached the front porch. A stocky, determined-looking woman with sturdy arms and legs, she stopped and stared in amazement, first at the finely dressed men standing in front of her and then at the crowd assembled behind them. The children cautiously peeked their heads from behind her cotton trousers.

'We are looking for Mr Yu,' An Ho announced.

Shooting a puzzled glance at Zhou Shi, she quickly wiped her hands on the spattered apron on her waist, took it off and absent-mindedly fixed her hair. 'One moment, please,' she said and went into the house, leaving the children open-mouthed for a second before they ran after her.

Yu appeared a few moments later, a swarthy man with a wart on his chin that sprouted a few long hairs. 'Why did you not ask them in?' he shouted back into the house before stepping forward. 'Hello. I am Yu,' he said with a bow. Yu suddenly became aware of the villagers standing a number of steps beyond the men and changed his tone. He also noted the quality of his guests' suits. 'Will you do me the honour of your presence in my humble home?' he asked.

'That will not be necessary,' said Chan.

'To what do I owe the pleasure?' Yu asked, glad to be seen talking to these men.

'I hear you have found something of historical interest,' Chan answered. 'A carved ball.'

'Ah, yes,' Yu replied, rubbing his hands together. 'I decided to go a bit beyond my usual fishing grounds – all the way to the Shengsi Islands. Had to spend the night there, in one of the abandoned huts.' He chuckled, warming to his story. 'When I brought up my net, it was—'

'I would like to see it,' Chan said in a quiet but insistent tone. 'To ascertain its authenticity, if you will.'

Yu shouted back into the hut for his wife. 'Bring me the thing I found.'

A muffled call came from inside the house.

He turned to face Chan. 'Just a moment, gentlemen. I shall have it for you to view presently.' He smiled at the men in front of him and lowered his voice. 'The others,' he whispered, indicating with his eyes the villagers standing at a respectful distance behind Chan, 'haven't had more than a glimpse of it. I wouldn't dare. I keep it where I found it. They may look good-natured, but they are a right bunch of thieves.'

Yu leaned back, smug, convinced of his superiority. 'Go mend your nets!' he shouted at the rabble outside, his voice full of condescension. He looked at Chan and gave a small wink.

Chan took no great pleasure in looking into other people's minds. Minds filled with the smallest of aspirations, the most fleeting of desires. The greed spilling across the fisherman's face, his crafty scheming and self-important posturing were so evident only a fool would fail to notice. It was clear he saw no value in the object other than how much he could get for it, hadn't a glimmer of interest in its real worth.

Yu's wife came forward, carrying a large, flat dish draped with a towel. Whatever was below the towel was heavy – Yu's wife was red-faced. Yu took a small, bone-handled knife from the scabbard dangling from his belt with one hand, and with the other gripped the towel and peeled it back. 'As soon as I saw it in its belly, I stopped cutting and left it alone – just as Zhou Shi instructed. I knew he was on the lookout for something out of the ordinary, though he never did say what exactly.'

Ignoring the blabbering old man, Chan leaned forward and gasped as his mind tumbled back to the vision he had seen in Pythias's house in Athens.

Below the towel was a sturgeon, its head and tail gone, the middle portion of its belly strangely swollen. Protruding through a single cut, like some strange, alien beast, was a sliver of green jade.

The second vision – the fish!

'Look at that! It's one big piece of jade, eh? How much do you think it's worth? A fortune?' Without waiting for an answer, Yu began slicing through the rest of the flesh around the ball. 'My nets are strong. Just as well. Such a weight of fish!' Yu chuckled, continuing to cut until, a moment later, with a sucking sound, the ball was free. 'There it is!' said Yu, holding it up in front of his face with one hand, and wiping the ball of fish innards. 'Amazing, eh?'

'Give it to me,' Chan said, thrusting out a hand.

Yu, eyes narrowing, smile gone, lowered the ball. 'We need to talk about the price—'

An Ho moved so quickly, Yu only realised the ball had been taken from him when he saw Chan grin. An Ho ordered Zhou Shi to find some water, which he brought in a wooden bucket. With Chan leaning over his shoulder, An Ho dipped the ball in the water and washed it, rinsing away the remaining gunge and lessening the stench of fish. That done, he handed the ball to Chan with a bow.

Chan knew as soon as he touched it. The ball pulsed, a hum vibrating through his fingertips.

Chan nodded to An Ho, who opened the suitcase, reached in, and dropped four thick wads of 100 yuan notes into the fisherman's clasped hands. As sunlight dappled the man's astonished face, Chan caught the man's thoughts: *More! He's rich, ask for more!* Chan nodded again and An Ho dropped four more onto the small pile.

'And the others,' Chan said, gazing at the open-mouthed crowd around him.

An Ho reached once more into the suitcase, and pulled out handful upon handful of notes, tossing them into the air and watching as the crowd rushed in, stepping over one another to scoop them up.

Chan walked back to the limo all the while mesmerised with the Jade Dragonball in the palm of his hand. Finally, the prize was his! Finally, Project Tian Shan could begin in earnest.

Zhou Shi, running ahead of Chan, reached the car and bowed deeply, opening the door. Chan paid him no mind. He climbed in and placed the Dragonball on the seat beside him. Zhou Shi was about to close the door when Chan stopped him.

'Get in,' he said to Zhou Shi.

For a moment, Zhou Shi hesitated. Had he heard correctly? Deciding he had and apologising profusely, he climbed in next to Chan and the Jade Dragonball. A moment later, An Ho joined them, sitting opposite them and placing the now empty suitcase at his feet.

The limo slowly pulled onto the gravel road and climbed up the mountain towards the pass. Chan continued staring vacantly out the window whilst his hand wandered to hover over the Jade Dragonball. Zhou Shi, afraid to speak, looked at the empty fields. The rice had recently been harvested and they stood bare.

'Your loyalty and perseverance have earned you a place in the inner circle, Zhou Shi.' Chan reached for a side panel and pressed his forefinger against it. An infra-red scanner identified the fingerprint and a secret drawer popped open. Within were bundles of newly minted bills, neatly stacked. Chan picked up a bundle and handed it to Zhou Shi.

'You have done well. However, I find your smell revolting. Make sure you wash as soon as we get to Shanghai. We are flying there immediately.'

'Shanghai,' Zhou Shi whispered, watching Chan's face.

Like an eager dog, thought Chan. *Once, a long time ago, his ancestors would have been powerful men, the associates of great lords. And now? Well, soon he would have a chance to be great again, make his ancestors proud...*

Chan rubbed his cheek, realising – with a chuckle – that it was hurting because he had been grinning so much. Straightening his face, he said, 'Yes, Shanghai. We shall return to the helicopter and fly there. Now that I have the Dragonball, there is someone there I wish to recruit. An Ho, see that there is a car waiting for us when we land in Shanghai.'

An Ho nodded. A few quick phones calls, and he had arranged a car. 'Boss,' he said, putting away his phone and looking sheepish. 'Very sorry – it's the marathon there today. Lots of roads closed.'

Chan shrugged dismissively at the possible delay the race would cause. *The finishing line for my own marathon is surely in sight.*

PART 2

HOBOKEN AND NEW YORK, USA — THE PRESENT DAY

CHAPTER 6

—

The windows looking out on the garden were hazy with condensation from the cold pressing up against them in the falling darkness. It would snow soon. Not that Sanjeev cared. It was 6pm; a Wednesday evening, and he was warm and cosy, sitting at the dining table getting ready to eat dinner. On the other side of the open-plan kitchen decorated in Matisse yellows and blues, his mother clattered pots and stirred sauces. Below the table, Jigsaw – a hairy black and brown mix of spaniel, terrier and who-knew-what – lay curled like a crescent moon, lightly snoring. In front of him, Sanjeev's father sat, grinning widely, still dressed in the suit he'd worn to the office. There at Brisk Airlines, he was an SVP, a super valuable person, or so he liked to say.

Sanjeev watched his father, who slackened his tie and undid the top button of his shirt. Something was going on. Exactly what it was, Sanjeev had no idea, but his father had one of those looks on his face – the one when his father was about to crack a joke or issue a challenge. Sanjeev pushed his glasses onto the bridge of his nose.

'I have something for you,' his father said. 'I think you'll like it.'

Sanjeev nodded. 'Two million dollars?'

'Nope.'

'My own time machine?'

'Nope.'

'Boots for Jigsaw?'

His father laughed. 'Nope. You want to see what I do have?'

'Sure.'

Like a bad magician, his father gave a little cough, jiggled his eyebrows, reached into his jacket pocket, and began rummaging about as though the pocket was a metre deep. Then he pulled something out of it and waved whatever it was back and forth. A moment later, he slid two tickets across the kitchen table, released them, leaned back, and grinned some more.

As soon as Sanjeev saw them, he knew what he *thought* they were – his father had mentioned buying them a few weeks ago.

'They won't bite, I promise,' he heard his father say.

Sanjeev stared at the two orange tickets in front of him. He wanted to believe his eyes; he really, *really* did.

'Go on,' his father said. 'They're yours.'

Slowly, Sanjeev leaned forward, afraid that if he moved too quickly, the tickets might flutter into the air and float away. Between his thumb and index finger, he rubbed the tickets together, heard them rustle. They were thin and smooth and shiny – and real!

'No way!' Sanjeev whispered.

'Way!' said his father, laughing.

Sanjeev raised the tickets and read what was printed on them.

Planet Odyssey: Voyage to New York
Saturday 12th November

'Seriously?' he asked, peering into his father's face.

'Seriously,' replied his father.

'YES!' Sanjeev cried, jumping up from his wooden chair and pumping his arms in the air. 'Oh man, oh man! YES!' He pointed at Jigsaw, who had woken up and was standing, wagging his tail madly. 'I'm going to experience *Planet Odyssey* in real life!' he cried. Grabbing Jigsaw's front paws, he began dancing him around in circles while Jigsaw hopped and barked.

Sanjeev grinned and sat down. Jigsaw started chasing his tail until Sanjeev patted him and told him to calm down too. When all were calm, Sanjeev's dad spoke again. 'The convention's actually for three days, but Friday and Sunday were fully booked, so I just got tickets for the Saturday…'

Sanjeev nodded. His head was buzzing. He was barely listening. Three more days, then the *Planet Odyssey* convention in New York – only twenty minutes away by car. Unreal!

Sanjeev's mother called from the other side of the room. 'Dinner will be ready in a minute. Sanjeev, could you take that book through to the sitting room please and come back for the salad?'

Sanjeev picked up his mother's thick book – *Art and Illusion* by E H Gombrich – from the cushion on the empty chair next to his father and carried it to the coffee table next door. Sanjeev recognised the author. He'd written *The History of Art* and *A Little History of the World*, books he enjoyed dipping into occasionally. His mother gave lectures at Rutgers University on art history when she wasn't managing her art gallery in town.

When he returned to the kitchen, his mother said: 'Toss the salad with vinaigrette and take it over, would you?' She smiled. Her dark brown, wavy hair looked particularly shiny under the bright kitchen lights.

As Sanjeev carried the salad to the table, his mother said, 'I have some good news as well. Uncle Manoj will visit tomorrow! He's finally taken some time away from his practice, but there's a conference in California he's speaking at on Saturday, so he can't stay here long.'

Sanjeev's eyes widened. *Uncle Manoj is coming here!* It had been such a long time since he'd seen his mother's elder brother. Every time they were in London, his uncle was somewhere else in the world, giving lectures and attending conferences. Uncle Manoj was a famous cardiologist. All that travel, not to mention being able to help so many people, made his job sound great... except for one thing: cardiologists dealt with an *awful* lot of blood. *Ugh!*

'Mom...' Sanjeev said hesitantly. 'Can I take the day off school tomorrow?'

His mother and father looked at one another.

'He never gets to see Manoj...' his father said.

His mother frowned. 'Let me think about it.'

Sanjeev grinned all the way upstairs after dinner: he knew his mother. A 'think about it' was as good as a 'yes'. Later in bed, he was still grinning: how cool to be going to the *Planet Odyssey* convention *and* get a day off school to see Uncle Manoj. Even better, Friday was November 11th – Veterans Day. The public holiday meant he could spend even more time with Uncle Manoj!

CHAPTER 7

'Sanjeev, please make sure you take care of Jigsaw after breakfast,' his mother called from downstairs. 'He needs his nails clipped – he's been sliding all over the floor. It would be great if you could do it before your uncle gets here.'

'Can't you do it, Mom?' Sanjeev shouted down to her.

'No, it's time you learned to care for him properly.'

'Yeah, I know, but—'

'Just do it, okay?'

Sanjeev groaned and continued rummaging around for Jigsaw's favourite toy: a yellow plastic duck that made a high-pitched squeak when it was squeezed. Where was it? Jigsaw was always leaving it in strange places. His head was under his bed when his mother called up again. 'And make sure you watch out for the quick of his nail. Now come down and get something to eat.'

'Okay, okay,' Sanjeev called, trying not to get a mouthful of dust bunnies. It had been a long time since he'd last looked under there, let alone cleaned, and it was hard to tell exactly what he was looking at. He pulled out a shoebox, blew the layer of dust off the lid and opened it. Inside were all of his Pokémon cards, separated into categories held together by rubber bands. He closed the box and was reaching for another – this one full of Lego pieces – when he saw what he was looking for wedged behind a pile of his old comics. 'Gotcha!' he cried, pulling the duck out by its bill.

'Sanjeev!'

'Coming!' he cried, and throwing the plastic toy onto his bed, he raced out of the room.

After his bowl of Lucky Charms, Sanjeev got the nail cutters from the cabinet under the sink.

'C'mon, Jigsaw!'

Jigsaw did not come. *That dog's no dummy,* Sanjeev thought. He knew he was going to get his nails clipped and was hiding.

With a pang of guilt, Sanjeev went to his room and slid the nail clippers under the bed where they wouldn't be seen and called Jigsaw again, making his voice sweet this time. 'C'mon, Jigsaw, I've got something for you!' He squeezed the plastic duck, making it squeak – once, twice, three times. Sure enough, Jigsaw's nails clicked on the stairs as he bounded up to Sanjeev's room. Sanjeev closed the door behind him as Jigsaw came in and took hold of the dog's collar. Jigsaw immediately stopped wagging his tail, flattened his ears back, and sat down on the floor. Sanjeev sat down next to him and took out the clippers. Jigsaw gave him a reproachful look as if to say, 'Clipping my nails is one thing, but tricking me is quite another…'

'I know, I know,' Sanjeev said. 'I really don't want to do this either, but Mom says I have to.'

He picked up one of the dog's paws and slid one of his nails into the grooved blade. Snip! One down, fifteen to go. He remembered what his mother had said – something about being quick? – and tried to pick up the pace. *Snip! Snip!* When Sanjeev clipped the next nail, Jigsaw gave a sharp yelp and pulled away his paw. He struggled to his legs and limped over to the door, his tail low.

'What's the matter, boy?' Sanjeev asked, but he already knew. He looked down and saw a few drops of blood on the carpet. He felt a wave of nausea come over him.

'M-Mom,' he called weakly. He went to Jigsaw and held him in his arms. Struggling to keep hold of Jigsaw, he opened the door and called again. 'Mom!'

His mother, who had taken a day off from the art gallery, came up the stairs carrying a basket of laundry. When she saw Sanjeev, she put it down in the hall and entered the room.

A dotted trail of Jigsaw's blood stained the carpet. 'Oh, Sanjeev! What did I tell you? Poor thing.' She gently put her hand on the dog's head and took a firm hold of his collar. 'Now go and get the styptic pen from under the sink.'

'The what?'

'The styptic pen to disinfect the cut and stop the bleeding, you silly goose! It's a grey tube.'

Sanjeev found the pen and brought it back while his mother spoke quietly into Jigsaw's ear. 'When you clip his nails, you must make sure not to clip too far or else you will cut his quick.'

His mother took the tube, opened it, and tapped it so a bit of powder filled the mouth of the barrel. Then she placed the end of the tube against the injured claw and held it there.

'I thought you wanted me to do it quick,' Sanjeev said, his head down.

'No, silly – the quick is the name of the blood vessel in his claws.' She turned to him. 'Sanjeev, you can't be that scatterbrained!' She lifted the styptic pen and inspected Jigsaw's claw. 'I think the bleeding has stopped. Let's finish clipping the rest of his nails later, after he's calmed down.' She moved out of the doorway and Jigsaw hobbled out.

His mother stood and pointed to the carpet. 'Now go get a rag and some soapy water. You must clean up the blood before it dries, or it will be much more difficult to get out.'

Sanjeev felt his stomach heave again. 'Can you do it, Mom?' he asked quietly.

'I most certainly cannot,' she answered. 'Now hurry!'

CHAPTER 8

———

Sanjeev was upstairs, still trying to build up the courage to clean the patch of blood, when the doorbell rang.

Uncle Manoj!

He dropped the soapy rag, rushed out of his bedroom and peered down the stairs. Forgetting his injured claw, Jigsaw was barking wildly, trying to push through Sanjeev's mother's legs as she opened the door. And there was Uncle Manoj, a beaming smile on his face. Much taller than Sanjeev's mother and much slimmer than his father, Uncle Manoj was dressed in a sky-blue button-down shirt with black slacks. His thick grey hair was combed back. Sanjeev's mother gave him a big hug.

'Uncle Manoj's here, Sanjeev!' his mother called over her shoulder and put a hand on the dog's head and pushed him gently away. 'Jigsaw, down!'

As Sanjeev reached the bottom step, his uncle turned. 'Hello, dear nephew!' he cried. They shook hands and hugged at the same time.

'Come in! Come in!' Sanjeev's mother said and ushered Uncle Manoj into the living room.

Uncle Manoj smiled. 'Something smells good!'

'Ah!' his mother said, laughing. 'How you managed to arrive on the day I make biryani I will never know!'

Leaning towards Sanjeev, Uncle Manoj let his voice sink to a conspiratorial whisper. 'Don't tell your mother, but I asked Jigsaw to spy for me.' He reached down to pat Jigsaw on the head. 'But I see he's limping a little, no?'

Sanjeev felt his face flush with embarrassment. 'Yes, I—'

Uncle Manoj carefully lifted Jigsaw's paw and looked at it. 'Ah, the nail was snipped too far.' Sanjeev felt his uncle's eyes on him, and was grateful when Sanjeev's father came in, Uncle Manoj's suitcase in his hand.

'Make yourself comfortable, Manoj,' his father said. 'I'll put this in your room.' And lowering the telescoping handle, he picked the suitcase and took it upstairs.

'Tea?' Sanjeev's mother asked.

'Yes, please,' Uncle Manoj cried as she retreated and he sat down. 'You have a beautiful home, Gita! I am very sorry I haven't been able to make it here sooner.'

'I know,' Sanjeev's mother replied. 'It's been ages.'

'Yes, true,' Uncle Manoj said, nodding. He turned to look at Sanjeev. 'And look at you – how tall you are! You must be even taller than your father.'

'Not yet,' Sanjeev said, 'but I'm the tallest in my class.'

'You mean your class at university?'

Sanjeev was about to say he meant his middle-grade school, but then he saw his uncle was only joking, he laughed, and Uncle Manoj laughed too. 'I remember when I was fourteen, but that was a long time ago.' His uncle paused and his face became more serious. 'So, your mother tells me you love the sciences. Any chance of you going into medicine?'

Careful not to embarrass his uncle, he tried to put some enthusiasm in his voice. 'I've heard it's… it's very interesting. But—'

'But you are not sure? Let me guess,' Uncle Manoj said. He paused, taking a sip of tea. 'You are squeamish about seeing blood, eh?'

Sanjeev felt silly admitting it, but it was true. 'Yeah. I don't know why. I just…'

Uncle Manoj nodded. 'I completely understand.'

Sanjeev's father came and sat on the sofa next to Sanjeev's mother, opposite Uncle Manoj and Sanjeev.

'Lots of us in the profession go through that,' Uncle Manoj continued. 'But there are many kinds of doctors.'

'Yes, I know, but…' Sanjeev shrugged. 'I'm not sure what I want to be yet.'

'Do what you love, so you become *you*,' his uncle said, and while he sipped more tea and listened, Sanjeev told him about the *Planet Odyssey* convention and the characters he was expecting to see there.

'Can't you come?' Sanjeev asked his uncle, his voice rising in excitement. 'Maybe they'll be selling tickets at the door.'

His uncle sighed. 'I wish I could, but I need to attend the San Diego conference.'

Sanjeev smiled. 'Oh well. I'll make sure you're an expert on Vorts before you go.'

'Good,' Uncle Manoj said. 'Other than medicine, the only thing I really know well is cricket.'

'Ahh, cricket…' his father sighed. 'You have no idea how much I miss playing and watching the Tests. But, to be honest, it hasn't been the same since Sachin Tendulkar retired.'

Uncle Manoj's face lit up. 'Ah yes, the Master Blaster. Now that was a batsman.'

Sanjeev realised that, no matter how many times they had explained it to him, he still didn't understand the rules of cricket. He was thinking how much fun it was having his uncle in the house when he noticed the photograph.

On the coffee table in front of him, *Art and Illusion* by E H Gombrich was open at a brightly-coloured picture: a mosaic from the Byzantium period from Ravenna in Italy. In it, the Emperor Justinian was wearing a long, brown robe, sandals and a gold sash and holding a golden bowl. A group of about ten people were standing next to him, looking serious. Sanjeev stared at the emperor's pinched face and irritated expression. He'd come across the picture many times flicking through the book, but today was different. Today, the hairs on the back of his neck rose…

His uncle caught him frowning. 'So, young man – what are we doing tomorrow? What adventures are you taking me on?'

Sanjeev reached over, closed the book and glanced at his mother. Before she could reply, Sanjeev pipped in with, 'Liberty Science Centre?'

'You've been there half a dozen times this year already!' his mother exclaimed.

'But it sounds interesting,' Uncle Manoj said. 'And if Sanju wants to go to the science museum, let's do that.'

'Yessss!' Sanjeev hissed.

CHAPTER 9

—

The next day, Friday, was spent at the Liberty Science Centre. As always, it was awesome – the planetarium, the exhibition about black holes, the 3D cinema theatre. Before Sanjeev knew it, it was dark outside and time for his uncle to catch his plane to San Diego.

Traffic on the highway to Newark Airport had been terrible – sleet had fallen, slowing everyone down – and it seemed like everyone in New Jersey needed to catch a plane that night. Nevertheless, they got there on time, parked their car, and accompanied Uncle Manoj while he checked in and walked towards the departures area.

As Sanjeev strolled along, listening to his uncle and carrying his uncle's smart, black briefcase in one hand and a bottle of water in the other, he caught a glimpse of his reflection in the shiny glass walls leading to the security area.

Like a trail of smoke, something dark – a long, swirling shape – was following him, lingering behind his head. He swivelled sharply. As he turned, he felt his body pitch forward and shed all its weight. He was falling, tumbling down, down, down. A terrific confusion of whites and blues made him close his eyes. He cried out, but the sound was muted, like a pillow had been put over his mouth. A soft wetness surrounded him. He opened his eyes and gaped at what he saw.

He was in water – deep, deep water – floating weightless like a piece of seaweed, but still able to see his arms and legs. He looked up. The surface, a shade lighter, was miles above his head. But somehow it didn't matter: he could breathe.

How is this possible?

He raised his arms, kicked his feet. He bobbed a little higher. He opened his mouth. 'Help!' he cried, bubbles pouring from it like a stream of giant pearls.

No help appeared.

What was I expecting? he asked himself. *A submarine?*

His calmness surprised him. Then again, what good would it do to get freaked out? Still, it was a violation of every scientific principle there was, as far as *he* knew. But it could be worse – the water could be cold!

He looked around while his hair swayed and his limbs gently rose and fell. There was nothing but murky blue with loads of little particles he thought might be plankton suspended in it. He blew another stream of pearly bubbles, laughing as they brushed past his nose and tickled it.

'This is awesome!' he cried. But then he closed his mouth. What if his supply of oxygen was somehow limited?

I should try to reach the surface, he decided, looking up at the faint light way above him. He was raising his arms, getting ready to propel himself upwards, when he saw the shape.

At first, he thought it was a shark, or even a torpedo – it was approaching so fast. It was long, but it wasn't sleek, he could see that now. And it definitely wasn't made of metal. Instead, it was ragged… and flapping… and – Sanjeev stared in shock – smiling.

A boy with hair swept back and wide-open eyes was swimming towards him. His feet were paddling at incredible speed, driving him through the water faster than any propeller ever could. Sanjeev circled his arms, trying to scoop away water, desperately wanting to move himself backwards.

It was useless.

A moment later, he was nose-to-nose with the boy, with nowhere to look but into the boy's eyes, which were as dark as night. For a second, the two boys remained that way: floating, each staring at the other. Then the boy with black eyes raised his hand and with a slow motion gently poked Sanjeev in the chest. As he did so, Sanjeev saw writing – a tattoo, perhaps – on the boy's arm. A barrage of bubbles burst out of the boy's mouth, but there were words too, though they were muffled by the water.

'You need the gills. They are important for you. Take them,' the boy said softly.

Sanjeev's eyes widened. Had he misheard? 'Gills? What are you talking about? What gills?' he cried, barely able to hear his words above the torrent of bubbles.

The boy leaned closer. His black eyes burrowed into Sanjeev's and his fingers tightened around Sanjeev's wrist. 'When the time comes,' he said, 'take the gills.'

Sanjeev instinctively pulled his arm away from the boy's grip.

The boy released Sanjeev's wrist, gave a sudden kick of his feet and zoomed away from Sanjeev, shrinking and shrinking into the gloom until…

'Hello? Hello, Sanju? Can I have my briefcase, please?'

Sanjeev opened his eyes and coughed, letting loose a spray of water.

'Hey! Watch the suit, Sanju!' his uncle cried, jumping back and laughing.

'What's the matter?' his mother asked, placing a hand on Sanjeev's forehead as she always did when she suspected he had a temperature.

'Water,' spluttered Sanjeev, turning his head left and right, trying to get his bearings. His family were looking at him with puzzled frowns. 'Went down the wrong way.' He coughed again and handed the briefcase to his uncle.

His father stretched out a hand and shook Uncle Manoj's other hand. 'I'm so glad you could make it, Manoj. We have missed you. Speaking with you has reminded me how much I miss discussing cricket. India versus England is coming up soon, isn't it? I'd love to visit Lord's,' his father said.

'I'd really enjoy taking you, Ravi! That's definitely on the list when you visit us in London this summer.' Uncle Manoj turned. 'Thank you, Gita. It was so good to see the three of you after such a long time.' He held up a bag that smelled of biryani. 'And thank you again for this. I will be the envy of rows three through seven.'

Sanjeev's mother gave Uncle Manoj a big hug. 'We'll see you again soon in London this summer,' she said, smiling.

Uncle Manoj nodded. He turned to Sanjeev. 'Now, young man, I hope you enjoy seeing the Jorts tomorrow.'

'Jorts?' Sanjeev asked, still half-dazed.

Uncle Manoj was about to reply when he caught sight of the time. 'Ah, it's always later than we think!' he cried, scooping up his luggage, holding his biryani high in the air, and smiling broadly at them. He showed his passport and boarding pass to the security officer, entered the security area, and – with a final wave and grin – disappeared.

A shudder jolted Sanjeev.

'Hey! Are you getting a cold?' his mother asked, wrapping an arm around his shoulders and squeezing him. 'You're trembling! What's the matter?'

Sanjeev tried to laugh it off. 'What? No, I'm totally fine.' He wriggled free, though his mother's eyes remained on him.

'Well,' said his father, looking grimly at the darkness pressing against the exit doors and pulling his jacket tight, 'once more unto the breach, dear friends and imitate the action of the tiger.'

His father always said this. According to him, it came from Shakespeare's *Henry V*, when Henry was encouraging his troops to be brave and attack the city walls of Harfleur. How terrifying war must be. But could it be any worse than that boy's cold, dark eyes? Sanjeev shivered again and swallowed. Was it something he'd eaten, a book he'd read, a film he'd watched? Sanjeev felt a dread and disquiet unlike anything he'd ever known in his fourteen years.

CHAPTER 10

‒

On Saturday afternoon, Sanjeev and his parents walked across the marble floors towards the reception desk. The large, rectangular lobby had a balcony running around the edge. A huge crystal chandelier hung from the gold ceiling. It dangled above a table on which was an arrangement of golden flowers in a tall vase. There were smart-looking dark leather couches and chairs. It was busy and noisy, and Sanjeev loved it. Just about everyone was wearing a *Planet Odyssey* outfit or was dressed as a member of an alien civilisation. There were purple-faced Zorians, pink-skinned Raarians with their ridges and their crests, blue-skinned Nebulists, Kog drones oozing wires, and of course lots of Vorts and their biological cousins, the Torts. And Urgons, the fiercest warriors in the universe. So cool!

'Your luggage will be sent to your rooms shortly,' the receptionist said, smiling. 'Is there anything else I can help you with today?'

'No, thank you,' Sanjeev's father replied.

The receptionist handed the room cards to Sanjeev's mother. 'In that case, we hope you enjoy your stay at the Wyndham New Yorker, Mr and Mrs Roy. You too, Sanjeev and Jigsaw.'

Sanjeev smiled and Jigsaw wagged his tail.

Two hours later, Jigsaw was upstairs in the hotel room, curled on Sanjeev's mother's lap while she read one of her favourite books, *Ways of Seeing*, and Sanjeev and his father were in the lift, dressed in their costumes, descending towards the foyer.

'Ready?' Sanjeev's father asked, his Blata costume making him look, Sanjeev thought, like a giant, hairy turtle.

'Yup!' replied Sanjeev, admiring himself in his blue, yellow and black *Endeavour* commander's uniform.

The lift doors slid open. A surprised couple jumped back. Sanjeev's father mumbled 'sorry' and shuffled past them.

'So,' his father said, his fake feet slapping on the marble floor as they crossed the lobby towards the exit, 'let's grab a taxi and warp factor twelve to the convention! Whadayasay?'

Sanjeev nodded. He smiled. It was a nice try, but the maximum speed of any Galactic Alliance ship was only warp nine-point-nine!

After Sanjeev's father had paid the taxi driver and put on the upper part of his costume again – it had been too big to wear inside the taxi – he and Sanjeev stood in the queue to enter the convention centre. Although there were lots of people, the lines were moving quickly.

When it was their turn, Sanjeev and his father gave their tickets to the security guards, bought a program, and walked into the main convention hall. What hit Sanjeev first was the noise and the enormity of the room. It was amazing. He had never seen anything like it. It was as though all the council members of the Galactic Alliance had gathered together in one place.

On the main stage to their left, an auction was underway. Sanjeev couldn't believe it. They were selling a pair of Mr Spartak's gills. Mr Spartak was a Vort, and Vorts could breathe in water and in air. Along with the gills, there was a signed photograph of Lester Nyman, the actor who played Mr Spartak. Amazing! The bidding was crazy. It had started at one thousand dollars and was rising by hundreds and hundreds of dollars every moment. Everybody wanted them.

Sanjeev froze.

When the time comes, take the gills.

The words floated in Sanjeev's mind. That's what that boy had said. What did it even mean? Were these the gills he meant? Even if he wanted to, how was he supposed to take them? Make a bid? Should he ask his father? The boy had said the gills were important for him. Even as all this flitted through, he knew it was madness to even think this. He didn't have $250 never mind $2,500, which was the price the bidding was currently at – and getting higher all the time.

Sanjeev shrugged. He wasn't going to let some weird hallucination spoil his fun. He turned to his right. In another corner of the giant hall, there was a separate exhibition. A three-metre replica of a door from the spaceship *Endeavour* was opening and closing as people entered it. As it did, Sanjeev caught glimpses of something inside. It was dark and glowing, pulsing red and blue. He saw the posters: Sets from *Planet Odyssey the Original Series.* The entire control deck from the *Endeavour* was on display! Sanjeev realised he was seeing the captain's chair, and the science and communication consoles every time the door slid open!

Sanjeev's father tapped Sanjeev's shoulder. 'Later, okay?'

'Really?'

'Yup, first we need to go over there.' Sanjeev's father pointed towards the side of the hall. 'Come on. We've got to hurry.'

Sanjeev followed. His father was leading him towards a long queue. Because his father was so busy trying not to bump into people with his costume, he didn't see the tall woman with long, dark hair who was causing a stir. But Sanjeev did. The woman, he immediately realised, was Alia Savio, who played Security Officer Zafira Grait in *Planet Odyssey, the Original Series.*

'Wow!' Sanjeev whispered as he watched her sweep past. She was the first famous person he had ever seen in real life.

'Here's the ticket,' his father said.

Sanjeev read it.

Photograph with Wallace Savage
Saturday 12th November
3.30 pm

'What, now?' Sanjeev said. 'I'm going to get my photograph taken with Wallace Savage now?'

'Yes! Now,' replied his father.

'Excellent,' Sanjeev breathed.

CHAPTER 11

＝

Sanjeev entered a small room where two white plastic chairs sat in front of a dark curtain. All around and above the curtain were studio lights. A tripod and a camera pointed at the chairs. On one chair sat Wallace Savage. Dressed casually in a smart blazer and white open-neck shirt, he was chatting to the photographer. When he saw Sanjeev, he stood up. 'Young man!' he said in his famously booming voice, grabbed Sanjeev's hand, and shook it hard.

Sanjeev stared at Wallace Savage. Sanjeev opened his mouth to speak. He wanted to tell Wallace Savage what an excellent actor he was, how happy he was to meet him, how surprised he was when his father told him he was coming to the convention… But the only thing he could think was how unbelievably white and regular his teeth were!

'Look here!' the photographer called. Sanjeev turned. He had just enough time to push his glasses onto the bridge of his nose when the studio lights flashed, once, twice, three times. Sanjeev blinked. Wallace Savage grabbed Sanjeev's hand again.

'Great! Thanks for coming here today. May you always endeavour!' he cried.

Sanjeev, too stunned to reply and half-blinded by the flash, grinned back stupidly. The next thing he knew, someone was giving him a token, and he was being led out of the room to meet his father again, passing the next person to be photographed.

And just like that, it was over.

An hour later, after he had visited the exhibition on the deck of the *Endeavour*, Sanjeev exchanged the token for his photograph with Wallace Savage. Yes, he had groaned because of the dorky expression on his face, and yes, he had wished he had brushed his hair before having the photograph taken because a loose strand had stuck straight up and made him look as though he had sprouted an antenna – but he didn't really care. All that mattered was that he had stood beside the one and only Wallace Savage, captain of the *Endeavour*. How cool was that? He couldn't wait to show it to Anton, Jermaine and Basem – his best friends at Jefferson High School. They were also sci-fi fans and would freak out when they saw it! The photo was going up on his wall, for sure, right above his model of the *Endeavour*.

'It's warm in here,' his father complained, wiping sweat from his forehead. 'This costume seemed like a good idea at the time, but it weighs a ton. You wanna get something to drink?'

'Sure,' replied Sanjeev, and, following his father much more closely this time, they made their way through the crowds towards a small drinks stall in front of which were three garden tables each with three plastic chairs. By chance, as Sanjeev and his father approached, the people sitting at one of the tables stood up. The man had a bullet-shaped head and a body with muscles that were so huge, Sanjeev thought they were fake. The boy with him, tall like Sanjeev with spiky brown hair and loads of spots, was dressed in an all-in-one silvery costume. He took two steps away from the table; then froze, turned around, and grabbed his drink. Sucking on the straw and making a sound like a drain, he emptied the cup, threw it onto the table, and dashed after his father. The cup bounced and fell onto the ground.

'Grab those seats,' his father whispered in Sanjeev's ear. 'I'll get our drinks.'

Sanjeev ran over and sat down, giving his father gave him a thumbs up. As he waited, a tide of aliens and humanoids of all shapes and sizes flowed past him. He'd been grinning ever since he had come into the convention centre and now, with his picture of Wallace Savage safely tucked in the bag they had given him, he was grinning even more. He glanced over at his father. He was standing in line, still waiting to be served. The Blata costume was dangling from his back like a huge, cheesy lasagne. Sanjeev chuckled. This was fun.

Over the public address system, someone was talking about a panel discussion that was about to begin called Multiverses: a solution to the Grandfather Paradox. Sanjeev wondered what they might do next. *Maybe check out the merchandise stands?* he was thinking when movement from the queue caught his eye. His father was waving at him. Sanjeev looked over. His father was pointing to a sign reading, *Rigel Juice: the Galaxy's Best Thirst Quencher*. Below the words was a picture of a tall glass filled with blue liquid. Sanjeev's eyes widened. He nodded. 'Yes, please!' he mouthed and turned back to the table.

And that's when he caught sight of the black and white framed photograph, lying flat on the chair closest to him. Sanjeev looked around. No one was paying him any attention: the river of people was still passing, his father was still staring into space, waiting.

Sanjeev leaned forward and took hold of the plastic chair. Gently, he pulled it away from the table, watching as more and more of the photograph was revealed until – Wow! He was looking at a portrait of Mr Spartak, with Lester Nyman's name signed in white pen below it. But that wasn't all. Below the signature, the same size and colour as several tortilla chips, were Mr Spartak's gills! Or to be more precise, the flesh-coloured, triangular rubber pieces that made Lester Nyman look like a water-and-air breathing Vort. Sanjeev's mouth fell open. The kid who had been sitting here before they arrived must have bought Mr Spartak's gills at the auction and left them by mistake!

Chapter 12

—

Sanjeev sat heavily on the seat. For the briefest of moments, he saw the framed photograph with Mr Spartak's gills on his bedroom wall, above the *Endeavour* and next to his Wallace Savage portrait. *I could slip it into my bag and walk out. No one would ever know. But I'd have to keep it in a secret place, one that only I knew...* He picked up the frame and stared at the gills.

When the time comes, take the gills.

Take the gills.

The boy's words echoed into Sanjeev's head along with the image of the boy's dark, unsettling eyes. Sanjeev rested the picture and the gills on his knees. *But what if I had been the one who had lost them? How would I feel?* he asked himself. He nodded. It was really tempting... but none of this belonged to him. Simple as that.

Just then, his father arrived with a tray carrying two drinks. 'Rigel juice, for two!' he said, laying the tray on the table and sitting down on the edge of his seat so there was room behind him for his costume.

'Look what I found,' Sanjeev said, placing the signed picture and the gills on the table.

'Weren't those—?'

'In the auction? Yeah. The people who were here must have left them. Is there a lost property office or something around here?'

'Actually, there's a security guard. Hey!' Sanjeev's father called, standing up and beckoning towards a woman who was wearing a dark blue uniform with a cap and black boots. 'Excuse me!' The woman looked over. 'Hi, yes. Can you help us, please?'

The woman strode over; Sanjeev's father quickly explained what had happened and the woman was talking into her walkie-talkie when—

'Hey!'

Sanjeev looked up. The boy and his father who had been sitting at the table were striding towards him. The boy, his mouth twisted in anger, the spots on his forehead flaming red, was staring angrily at Sanjeev.

'We were just—' began Sanjeev.

'About to steal them,' the boy said, snatching the framed photo and then the gills from Sanjeev's hands. 'These cost three-thousand bucks!'

'Honestly, I wasn't—'

'Hey, man,' the boy's father said, stepping forward and pushing his chin out at Sanjeev's father, 'what's the deal?'

Before Sanjeev's father could answer, the security guard said, 'These people have filed a report about lost property. Are you saying this property is yours?'

'Yeah!' the man cried. 'This stuff is ours! We paid for it, okay?' He waved a receipt in her face.

'Just calm down, sir. Nobody's saying it isn't. If you'll come with me, we can sort it all out, alright?' The woman looked at Sanjeev and smiled. 'But if I were you, first I'd say thank you to this guy for finding it.'

The boy took one look at Sanjeev and spat, 'Yeah, right!' Then he turned to his father. 'Let's go! There are too many thieves around here.'

The boy's father gave Sanjeev and his father a long, hard stare then walked away too.

The security guard shrugged apologetically and silently mouthed the word 'sorry'.

'Don't worry about it,' Sanjeev's father said. 'No harm, no foul.'

After they had gone, Sanjeev's father picked up his drink. 'Guaranteed to make your tongue turn blue or your money back!'

Sanjeev smiled. Taking his plastic cup, he pushed the straw into it and took a mouthful of the sweet, blue juice. It tasted horrible – like toothpaste. As he sipped and as his father gulped, Sanjeev thought about what had happened. What if he had taken the gills? The boy and his father were so angry and aggressive. Would they have become violent? Tried to beat them up? Would they have called the police and had them arrested? Whatever might have happened, none of it would have been good. Did the underwater boy want to get Sanjeev into trouble… maybe even get him or his father hurt? The thought puzzled and chilled Sanjeev… until he shook himself.

What nonsense am I thinking about? The underwater boy was a hallucination, dummy! And the gills? So easy to explain: he knew the gills were up for auction because he had read about it on the convention's website! His *mind* had made the boy talk about the gills because his *mind* had been playing tricks on him. The evil boy with evil plans was clearly a product of food poisoning after all. It was the only logical explanation.

'Done?' Sanjeev's father asked, his cup empty.

Sanjeev made a face. 'Do I have to finish it?'

'Of course not,' his father said and, reaching forward, he plopped a podgy hand on Sanjeev's head and messed up Sanjeev's hair. 'You're a good kid, you know that?' he said.

'Hey!' Sanjeev cried, pulling free and flattening down the wildest strands of hair. 'My hair looks bad enough already.'

'Yeah… You know, your hair sticking up like that? It sort of makes you look like a cockatoo!'

'Thanks, Dad. Thanks a lot.' His father's stomach was wobbling madly. Even Sanjeev had to laugh.

'Come on, kiddo,' his father said when they had stopped laughing. 'We've got a lot to do.'

CHAPTER 13

—

After they returned from the convention, his father decided to have a nap. Even though the door was closed, Sanjeev could hear his father's snores. *And he calls me a snorer!*

His mother, Jigsaw and he walked towards the lift, Jigsaw straining at the leash, practically choking himself.

'Easy!' Sanjeev told him. Jigsaw looked up and seemed to understand.

Luckily, there was a park nearby. Sanjeev had asked the concierge earlier where he could take Jigsaw for a walk. 'Try Bryant Park,' the concierge had told him. 'They allow dogs in there. It's easy to find, just go left at Port Authority and continue along 42nd Street until you see trees!'

The lift arrived with a *bing* and the three of them got in. Jigsaw began whining. 'Alright, Jig. We'll be there soon,' Sanjeev said.

'So, I hear you had a good time today,' his mother said.

'Really great,' replied Sanjeev.

'What did you like the most?'

Sanjeev thought about it. Meeting Wallace Savage was really cool, and so was seeing the *Endeavour's* bridge and engine room. Then there were all the people dressed as *Planet Odyssey* characters, and he loved staying in the Big Apple in his own room. It was tough to pick out one thing. 'I dunno,' he said. 'I liked everything.' *Everything except the thing with the gills*, he thought.

The lift doors slid open again. When they stepped out, the concierge gave Sanjeev a wave, which he returned. The lobby was much quieter now.

Outside, it was a clear, cold night. The streets were busy with traffic – bright headlights were zigzagging their way around town, and lots of people milled around. Everyone seemed to be in a rush to get somewhere. Sanjeev shivered as snowflakes brushed his cheeks. With his mother holding Jigsaw's lead, he quickly zipped up his jacket and pulled down his wool hat so it covered his ears, which were tingling with the cold. He could have kicked himself for forgetting his gloves.

'Any thoughts about what you'd like to do tomorrow?' she asked.

Sanjeev's father had already suggested visiting something that sounded pretty cool. 'The Intrepid Air and Space Museum's got 4D flight simulators,' Sanjeev said. 'Maybe we could go there.'

His mother smiled. 'Sounds good.'

They continued walking, their breaths making candy-floss clouds in front of them. They turned left at Port Authority and saw the trees that the concierge had talked about. A short while later, they entered the park from 42nd Street and followed a short path that led them through the trees towards a broad lawn.

'Nice,' Sanjeev said, stepping onto the grass. The trees surrounded it on three sides. On the fourth, there was a grand-looking old building lit up by spotlights. Above the trees on every side, skyscrapers loomed, standing like sentinels towering over the park.

'The New York public library looks good at night, doesn't it?' his mother said.

Sanjeev nodded. 'It was in *The Day After Tomorrow* – and the original *Ghostbusters*,' he said.

His mother chuckled. 'So it was.'

Jigsaw tugged at his lead, desperate to run free. Sanjeev wanted to let him have some fun, but it was against the park's rules – the concierge had warned him about that. All dogs had to be kept on a leash. Suddenly, Jigsaw caught a scent. His head swivelled. He rooted around, nose to the grass, trying to figure out which direction the smell led.

'Hey!' Sanjeev complained as Jigsaw suddenly lurched forward, almost pulling the leash from Sanjeev's hand. The dog ignored Sanjeev's cry. Instead, nose glued to the ground, head turning this way and that, he followed the scent, dragging Sanjeev across the grass towards the trees on the other side of the park.

'Stay on the lawn,' his mother called. Sanjeev looked back. She was already ten metres away, her face hard to see in the half-light.

'Okay,' Sanjeev cried. He was getting ready to dig his heels in and stop Jigsaw's mad dash when the leash fell slack. Jigsaw had frozen in concentration, staring hard at something in the trees.

Sanjeev peered into the shadows. 'What is it, boy?'

Jigsaw didn't move. Sanjeev continued to stare into the bushes and the semi-darkness there, trying to see what had interested his dog. And then he saw it. Or rather, them: three small shapes, standing on their hind legs, peering back at him, their slender ears like three Vs.

Three rabbits.

'Sanjeev?' his mother called.

He turned. 'Be there in a second,' he called. When he looked back, the three small, furry shapes had gone. 'Strange', he said to himself. But he had barely said it when a creeping fear rose in him. His heart beat harder. The darkness he was staring at grew deeper. Beside him, Jigsaw whimpered. Sanjeev looked on in horror: the same swirling smoke as he had seen at Newark Airport was pouring out of the bushes and gushing towards him. Before Sanjeev could do anything, it was licking the ground at his feet, engulfing his legs, his waist, his shoulders, his head. And then it was all around him and he was inside the smoke, and the bushes, the park, Jigsaw had all gone.

He coughed, looked left and right, up and down. Grey nothingness surrounded him. He opened his mouth to call for help. But the next second, the boy, the same one as before, appeared as if he had walked through a door in the greyness. His dark eyes locked on Sanjeev's and burrowed into them. Without a word, the boy raised his hand and a sneering grin spread across his face. Sanjeev gazed at the object it held, hardly believing what his eyes told him. Because there on the boy's palm was a small, yellow object in the shape of a duck, Jigsaw's favourite toy.

Without thinking, Sanjeev stepped forward to snatch the toy away, but the boy was too quick.

'What do you want?' Sanjeev asked, his voice quivering.

The boy snarled silently and rushed forward, stopping a centimetre from Sanjeev's face, close enough for Sanjeev to smell the stink of rotten fish and decomposing seaweed. From beneath a mop of shaggy black hair, the boy held Sanjeev's terrified stare and then, leaning back, he shifted his eyes to his hand. As Sanjeev watched, the boy curled his fingers, slowly closing them around the plastic toy. And as if the toy was made of cake, he crushed it, the crumbs and larger pieces squeezed out of the side of his hand and tumbled away.

'What…? What do you want?' Sanjeev cried.

But the boy wasn't listening. The mist had suddenly thinned, and like a strand of spaghetti, the boy's body had become elongated and thinner, as though he were being pulled feet first into a black hole. Sanjeev, stumbling away in horror, watched as the boy's hugely elongated face – a nose as long as a leg, a chin as long as an arm

– slid away and finally disappeared completely, replaced by the park's bushes.

When his mother asked him if he was alright, he jumped at least a metre. And although he managed to convince her that he was fine, all the way back to the hotel, there was one horrible, scary thought in his head: had that *thing* threatened Jigsaw?

PART 3

SHANGHAI, CHINA —
THE PRESENT DAY

CHAPTER 14

Nothing had ever stopped Lin Dan getting to his lab. Not the flu, not a flat tyre, not a dead car battery, not even the birth of his daughter, Yuqi – though admittedly he had left the lab early and rushed to the hospital just as his wife was about to give birth.

And the Shanghai marathon wasn't about to stop him either.

'But can't you take a day off?' his wife Mei said, standing at the door of their home with Yuqi in her arms. 'It's going to take you hours to get to the lab.'

Lin Dan smiled, kissed his wife's cheek and gave Yuqi a hug and kissed her too. She babbled delightedly, looking and sounding much happier than his wife. 'And it's a Sunday!' his wife cried, making a final attempt at persuading him to stay.

Lin Dan shrugged – a what-can-I-do expression on his boyish face. Work was work. He had had an idea last night that couldn't wait for Monday. He *had* to go to the lab. 'I'll see you later – six, maybe,' he said, taking out his car keys and grinning as his wife gently shook her head.

Two and a half hours later – a long time for a seventeen-kilometre journey but still faster than he expected – Lin Dan entered the campus of Shanghai Jiao Tong University. He walked into the tall, red brick and glass building where his lab was, offered his iris for scanning, nodded to the single security officer on duty, and, preferring the stairs, climbed them to the third floor.

Inside, his lab was silent but for the hum of the florescent lights. It was strange; Room 41 usually held twenty people, but Lin Dan treasured the quiet. After fighting his way through the traffic, he was tired. He closed his eyes for a moment and rubbed his temples, but his idea would not leave him alone.

Pulling on his white lab coat, he sat at his desk and peered at the model filling his computer screen: a 3D simulation of the building blocks of human life. Genes were important because they made proteins that were needed by the body. When there was a mutation, or unwanted change, in a gene, it produced a protein that didn't work properly. In the case of people who aged quickly, the abnormal protein had a terrible effect because it destroyed the body's cells.

Lin Dan was especially fascinated by a mineral called fingerite and its role in preventing or even reversing rapid ageing. The idea to look at the effects of fingerite had come from a research paper that had mysteriously appeared in his email inbox. But what Lin Dan couldn't figure out was how fingerite worked. The research paper had given no details.

What had occurred to him while he ate his breakfast that morning was instead of focusing on how the gene responsible for the mutation, influenced by fingerite, affected the body, he should concentrate on how other genes, influenced by fingerite, affected the gene responsible for the mutation – because that's what some genes did: they controlled others. He looked up at the white walls of the lab, concentrating on the problem, letting his mind travel inward…

The noise of a door slamming shut brought him back to Room 41. He swung his chair round and found himself looking at three men. A large one with square shoulders and a slender, young one stood either side of an older, smaller man who looked vaguely familiar. They were well-dressed, their faces impassive. They stood there silently for a moment, the older man staring intently.

'Lin Dan,' the older man finally said, his voice flat.

'C-can I help you?' Lin Dan asked, rising from his seat.

'As it happens, you can,' the older man said. 'And I, in turn, can help you.'

'I'm sorry, but who are you?' Lin Dan asked.

'Forgive me, I am being impolite,' the grey-faced, grey-haired man said. 'Perhaps you do not recognise me.' The man leaned in towards Lin Dan. 'My name is Chan.'

Lin Dan bowed stiffly.

'Please, please have a seat,' Chan said with a wave of his hand.

Lin Dan sat back down in his chair as the old man looked around the lab, his eyes lingering on the computer screens. He picked up a book atop the pile, read the cover, and leafed through the first few pages. At last, he turned back to face Lin Dan.

Lin Dan suddenly recalled that the person in front of him was the chairman of Bai Lu, and he wasn't seventy years old, he was seventeen. Chan had offered him a job in Xi'an and Lin Dan had turned him down – not once, but several times. There were rumours: that Chan was the head of a crime syndicate; that he dealt ruthlessly with those who disobeyed or displeased him. It would be dangerous to disappoint a man like him, Lin Dan had supposed. He had hoped Chan would forget about him. That was clearly a mistake. The room suddenly felt very small.

'What is it you want?' Lin Dan asked.

Chan smiled. 'I greatly admire your research, Dr Dan. I have been following your work with interest, and it is my opinion that your accomplishments as a bio-engineer have not received the recognition they deserve.'

'Thank you,' Lin Dan answered, caught off-guard by what seemed like genuine praise.

Chan continued. 'Bai Lu, my company, is beginning a new project in Xi'an. If you remember, we approached you earlier about a job there.'

'I remember,' Lin Dan replied, aware that sweat was pooling at the bottom of his spine and under his armpits.

'I am very keen for you to come and work for me. You will have access to a laboratory that far surpasses those you have worked in previously.' Before Lin Dan could fully process what he had said, Chan, his eyes still on Lin Dan, held out his hand, palm up. The heavy-set man beside him pulled open his suit, reached into the breast pocket inside, and took out a card. He placed it in Chan's hand and Chan slid the card onto the table in front of Lin Dan.

An icy chill ran through Lin Dan, and his stomach clenched like a fist, threatening to make him either shiver or throw up, he wasn't sure which. It was a photo of Mei and Yuqi.

'Such a beautiful family,' Chan said.

'How, how…' Lin Dan stammered.

Chan's eyes burned. 'Ah, we all have our ways, don't we?' He reached forward. Lin Dan flinched but tried to hide it. 'Here,' Chan said, pushing it towards Lin Dan. 'Consider it a keepsake. We have more of them. Some nice shots with your parents as well.'

Chan reached into the inside pocket of his suit and withdrew a gold case the size of a mobile. He opened it and took out a business card, which he slid onto the table in front of Lin Dan. The card had one word, *Bai Lu*, and a phone number.

'Please consider our offer – and the many advantages it is certain to bring you and your family. We will be back to hear of your decision… or perhaps you would prefer to call.' Chan rose and walked slowly to the door. Before he left, he stopped and turned back to the scientist. A cruel smile sat on his dry lips. 'Remember,' he said, 'a man who cannot tolerate small misfortunes can never accomplish great things.'

The three men had been gone less than five minutes when Lin Dan snatched the card and called the number. He was so hoarse, he barely recognised his own voice. 'I will do whatever you want. Just please leave my family alone. They are the most precious—'

A chuckle interrupted him. 'Yes,' said the voice of Chan, 'and that is how they will stay – precious – *if* you do exactly as I say.'

PART 4

HOBOKEN, USA –
THE PRESENT DAY

CHAPTER 15

—

Jigsaw was missing for three days. Three days! How could anyone survive that long without food and a warm place to sleep? Danny Myer's cat had been missing for nearly a month before he found it, but that had been in summer. Sanjeev swallowed hard – an image of Jigsaw wandering the snowy streets deepening his depression further.

'Don't give up,' Sanjeev's father had told him. He didn't plan to.

Sanjeev plodded slowly down the stairs; arms wrapped around his body. The scene in which he discovered the garden empty and Jigsaw gone played in his head for the thousandth time.

He had been upstairs, getting ready for school. He had been standing at his bedroom window when he had glanced out and seen his father leave, seen him close the front garden gate behind him. Then he had gone downstairs, said goodbye to his mother, left the house, gone along the path, closed the garden gate, met Anton, and – Sanjeev felt the emptiness in his stomach return – then he had returned to the house because he had forgotten his trainers for gym. He had rushed upstairs, grabbed them, ran out of the house, down the garden path, and…

He hadn't even been able to admit that it was his fault. That he had made a mistake. That Jigsaw hadn't disappeared into thin air. That some kid hadn't just walked past and decided to let his dog out. And his father definitely hadn't forgotten to close the gate. No, it was because of him. Jigsaw had run out of the garden because he, Sanjeev Roy, the worst dog owner in the world, hadn't shut the gate properly. This time, he would say it, tell his parents. He really would.

Another thought suddenly crossed his mind, filling him with doubt. *What if I haven't made enough posters?* Then it hit him. *I can find the local bulletin board – the town news, online. I can put info about Jigsaw on their website, maybe post a picture there. That'll be better than Snapchat.*

He turned and raced back upstairs. 'Be down in a minute,' he called. 'I've forgotten something important.'

He closed the door behind him, turned on the computer, waited a moment for it to boot up. He wondered what he could do to get more hits on the site. Maybe he could scan the poster…

The computer came on and he opened a browser. He was about to type in search terms for the town news when he noticed the computer screen looked a little… warped. Maybe it had sat in the sunlight too long. He ran his hand over the screen. No, it didn't feel warped. Sanjeev brought his face up to the screen and looked at it more closely.

The screen image itself seemed to be moving, swirling like thick fog. At first, it was formless, but after a bit, Sanjeev thought he could make out shapes.

And then, unmistakably, an eye.

Sanjeev stifled a scream and rolled his chair back, away from the desk. The eye stayed in placed, blinked once and disappeared. But then an ear appeared, and then another eye and a nose…

The face wouldn't stay in focus. Part of it would come clear, emerging for a moment from the fog, only to get swallowed up by it again. It looked like it was trying to push towards him. Trying to free itself.

Sanjeev watched in horror as the face turned this way and that, squirming like a lizard coming out of an egg. Each time it pushed, Sanjeev slid his chair back farther until he was pressed up against the opposite wall. He felt his arms and legs grow heavy, the strength draining from his body. The face disappeared entirely, until – WHAM! It smashed into the screen, causing a spiderweb of cracks to spread along its surface. For a few agonising seconds, Sanjeev watched helplessly as it thrashed about.

He recognised the face.

It was the boy.

All at once, the face stilled. The eyes, glowing with dark hatred, stared into his for one long moment, then disappeared.

Sanjeev realised he'd been holding his breath. He sat in stunned silence, waiting for his strength to return.

He wanted to believe it hadn't happened, but there they were – cracks in his monitor.

Sanjeev raced from the room, leaving the computer lying where it was. The boy he had seen underwater had just tried to escape from the computer screen; the last thing he wanted to do now was go anywhere near it.

CHAPTER 16

—

'Did you print the posters?' asked Sanjeev's father, chewing and speaking at the same time.

Sanjeev shook, unable to talk. Should he tell his parents about the boy? But that was stupid. It was all in his head, surely? Was he having hallucinations? Would he need to go to a psychiatrist? Was he hearing voices in his head? But what about the computer screen? Had it really cracked? Had he inadvertently cracked it?

He was trembling as he sat down at the breakfast table in his usual seat – the one that faced the kitchen window and gave a view of their small backyard and the fencing enclosing it. Before Jigsaw's disappearance, Sanjeev's mother had insisted that the dog be put in the backyard while the family ate their meals. When Jigsaw was outside, he would bounce around, occasionally whining, occasionally barking; then, when they finished breakfast and Sanjeev's mother opened the kitchen door, Jigsaw would rush in and gulp down any scraps in his bowl. No, the boy was his imagination, likely so was the computer screen cracking. And besides, he had something far more important to tell his parents, anyway. He needed to focus on reality and not get carried away by the craziness in his head right now.

Sanjeev stared out the window. There was no Jigsaw, just darkness. Sanjeev picked up his fork, then remembered his father's question. 'I printed twenty.'

His father nodded. 'We'll take them to Hamilton Avenue, put them on some trees there. Then we'll go down to Sam's grocery, ask them if they'll put a poster in their shop window. What do you say?'

Sanjeev gave a weak smile. *Say it,* he told himself. *Say it.*

His mother sat down, picked up her knife and fork and began eating. 'So,' she said, 'looking forward to the trip?'

The whole of Class 8 was going to the museum to see a special exhibition about the Silk Road and the ancient kingdoms it connected. They had been studying stuff like that in Mrs Milo's class: ancient China, silkworms, trade, the exchange of ideas and people. According to the teacher, silkworms were brought to the West for the first time after they were smuggled out of China. Some guy called Procopius wrote about it, she'd said. When Mrs Milo first told them about the trip, Sanjeev had been excited, just as his friends had been. But not now.

'Can I take the day off school?' Sanjeev asked.

For a moment, there was silence. Finally, it was his mother who spoke. 'Why?' she asked, her forkful of food poised in front of her.

'I want to take the posters down to Hamilton Avenue with Dad.'

Sanjeev's father coughed noisily and gulped down some tea.

'Can't you put up the posters *and* go to school?' his mother asked, waving the fork in the very general direction of Hamilton Avenue, then Jefferson High.

Sanjeev could see she was annoyed. He continued anyway. 'No, I can't 'cause the bus leaves Jefferson High at 9.30am and it's 7.25am now. I won't have time to put up the posters and catch the bus to the Met.'

'I see,' said his mother, putting the egg in her mouth and giving her husband a hard look.

His father coughed again. 'Er...' he said. 'Look. There's no point in both of us going down Hamilton Avenue. I can put up the posters myself. It won't take long. And it's freezing out there. Means only your old man gets frostbitten.' His father grinned.

It is freezing out there, thought Sanjeev. *And putting up the posters is all that really matters, right?* Another thought struck him too: if he didn't go to school, his parents would be angry. An argument was looming; he knew it. There was only one thing to do. 'Okay. I'll bring down the posters and you can put them up.'

Sanjeev watched as his parents continued their breakfast, eating it methodically and in silence. *Now isn't the time,* he thought. *But tonight, I'll tell them it was my fault. Definitely.*

So, make it definite! Say something! he told himself.

He cleared his throat, squirmed a little in his chair. 'I need…' He hesitated, changing his mind and then changing it back again. 'I need to tell you something.'

His mother and father looked up, puzzled.

'But tonight, okay?'

His father shrugged. 'Okay.'

'Okay,' his mother said.

'Okay,' Sanjeev said, suddenly feeling like a weight had been lifted. He needed to confess, tell his parents that Jigsaw's disappearance had been his fault.

CHAPTER 17

—

The icy wind was a punch in the face. Sanjeev shivered. His fleece was zipped all the way up to his neck, his parka was pulled tightly around his body, and he had on a hat, scarf and gloves. But he knew by the time he reached Jefferson High he would be about as warm as an ice cube. *Why can't we live in Florida or someplace warm like that?* he thought for the millionth time. He sighed, stretched his arms out like a high-wire walker, and started shuffling along the path. The icy frost beneath his feet sparkled and shone. A picture of Jigsaw alone in the dark streets slipped into his mind again. How cold he must be. Sanjeev looked up. A few more steps to the gate.

He thought about his father. He had already left the house, taking the bundle of posters with him and promising he would have them all up before he began work. Sanjeev reached out a gloved hand and took hold of the garden gate. He held on to it as he put first one foot, then the other onto the main street's pavement.

He made it. A moment later, he heard the key turn in his next-door neighbour's door. Anton appeared, frowning until he saw Sanjeev. 'Yo!' he called and Sanjeev, hands in white, knitted gloves, waved back.

Mistake!

A grin flashed across Anton's face. Sanjeev stuck his hands in his jacket pockets and watched as Anton turned, yelled goodbye to someone inside and slammed the door behind him. Anton stepped carefully along his garden path. It was icy too. Sanjeev watched Anton step gingerly onto the main street.

Any moment now, thought Sanjeev.

'Nice gloves, man,' said Anton, tightening his scarf and grinning. 'You make them yourself?'

'Don't be stupid,' replied Sanjeev.

'Bet they're warm, right?'

'They are, actually.'

'Mom make them?'

'Grandmother.'

'Huh. Any sign of him?'

Sanjeev didn't need to ask who 'he' was. He shook his head. There wasn't much that he and Anton had in common. Anton was loud – the class clown – or so Mrs Milo often said, and Anton was definitely not as massive a fan of *Planet Odyssey* – he thought *Star Drifter* was way better. Anton was also heavy – not fat, just square-shouldered, with thick arms and legs – whereas Sanjeev was slim. And Sanjeev wore glasses, whereas Anton didn't. But the biggest difference was that Anton was always getting into trouble. Truth was, if Anton hadn't been Sanjeev's next-door neighbour, and if Sanjeev hadn't had Jigsaw, they might never have been good friends. Anton loved Jigsaw almost as much as Sanjeev did.

For some reason, Anton's parents hated dogs and Anton would volunteer – volunteer! – to take Jigsaw for a walk, hail, rain or shine. Of course, Anton made Sanjeev laugh. That was another reason why they were friends, he had to admit that.

The boys walked on in silence and turned onto Borough Road, at the end of which was their school. The traffic was always heavier and noisier on this part of the road. Buses, cars and taxis choked it. This morning was no different. Cars crawled through a series of traffic lights and intersections. Headlights illuminated rising exhaust fumes. Brake lights radiated red. Horns blared. Sanjeev hated this part of the journey to school. At least there wasn't much snow on the pavement; mostly, it had slipped into the gutters or gathered against walls or in doorways. Sanjeev looked at his watch. 'Hey,' he said, pointing to it. It was almost 8.55am. They picked up their pace. 'Looking forward to the Met?' Sanjeev asked.

'Sure,' replied Anton. He grinned. 'Like a trip to the dentist.'

'Anita Perez?'

'Here!'

'Sanjeev Roy?'

'Here!'

'Valerie Shultz?'

'Here!'

The checking of the list continued until the teacher ticked everyone's name. Pen in mouth, Mrs Milo ran her finger down the list, counting silently. Then she counted the heads on the bus and nodded, satisfied. She opened her mouth to address everyone just as the bus driver revved the engine. Anton, sitting next to Sanjeev, sniggered. Mrs Milo shot him a look. Anton pulled as serious a face as he could.

'Now listen carefully, everyone. I want to remind you of our travel plans,' said Mrs Milo. 'Our bus this morning will take us to the PATH train station at Hoboken, which shouldn't take more than ten minutes. Once we get there, we'll take the PATH to 33rd Street, which is near Penn Station. Then we'll take the subway to 86th Street. We'll come out near 5th Avenue and walk to the Met. Once we're inside, we're going straight into the Silk Road exhibition. I want you to stay together. That means you walk with your group, travel on the subway with your group, enter the exhibition with your group, and return with your group. Are we clear?'

'Yes, Mrs Milo,' replied a chorus of voices.

The teacher gave them a wry smile and sat down. As soon as she did, excited conversations broke out everywhere. A moment later, the bus rolled forward and a huge cheer went up.

Two heads rose above the seats in front of Sanjeev and Anton – Basem and Jermaine. Although the four friends were all the same age, Jermaine was a head taller than the others, and Basem a head shorter. Jermaine's hair stuck out, making a perfect sphere around his skull, while Basem's was short and prickly.

'Hey, you find Jigsaw yet?' Jermaine asked.

Sanjeev shook his head.

'Oh man, that sucks!' Basem said.

'Basem and Jermaine,' came Mrs Milo's voice from the front of the bus. 'In your seats, please, and fasten your seat belts. That goes for everyone.'

Sanjeev did as he was told. With another roar, the bus rolled forward. Everyone cheered, except Sanjeev. When Anton saw this, he nudged his friend in the ribs. 'Come on. Cheer up. Enjoy the trip. Jigsaw'll turn up, you'll see.'

Sanjeev said nothing.

'Wanna watch some *Forensics Five-0*?' asked Anton, mobile in his hand. 'I can stream it on this.' The cop series was one of Anton's favourites. Whenever Sanjeev went to Anton's house, there seemed to be an episode playing. Either that, or it was something from *Star Drifter*.

Sanjeev shrugged.

'He says he's not guilty…' Anton said in a deep voice.

'…But the forensics say different,' Sanjeev said, completing the quote.

Anton laughed, and they settled back in their seats to watch Captain Max Eastern and his team of forensic investigators solve another case while the bus ploughed through the early morning traffic towards Hoboken station.

Chapter 18

—

When they arrived at Hoboken station, everyone clambered off the bus. It seemed even colder than before.

'Man, it's freezing,' Sanjeev said, tightening his scarf and then pulling on his gloves.

Anton looked at Sanjeev's gloves and smirked.

Ignoring Anton, Sanjeev was about to step through the doors of the station when he looked to his left and saw a woman on the ground, sitting with her back against the station's brick wall. In front of her was a piece of soggy cardboard on which words were written in red crayon letters. *Lost my job. Lost my home. Lost my family.* The woman was wearing layers and layers of clothes – her body was puffed up because of them. But even with all the clothes she wore, the woman still looked cold. Sanjeev wondered if her feet were wet because the soles of the shoes she was wearing were cracked. Next to the cardboard sign, there was a small collection of loose change. The woman lifted her chin, gazed at Sanjeev for a second, and looked down again. Sanjeev was surprised: the woman looked like anyone else on that street. 'How is it possible for such a rich country to allow such poverty?' Sanjeev's mother would always ask. As if Sanjeev had the answer.

Reaching into his coat pocket, Sanjeev tried to get hold of some change from his pocket. But before he could get any, something cold and hard smashed into the side of his head – BOOM!

Reeling, Sanjeev pulled his hand out of his pocket to steady himself and looked in the direction of where the missile had come from. Anton! He was standing and staring at Sanjeev with a stupid, surprised look on his face, as though hitting Sanjeev with the snowball from three metres away was a million-to-one shot, his whole face making a big O-shape. But that only lasted for a second, then Anton was doubled over and laughing so hard he sounded like he was choking. And not just him. The rest of Class 8 had got off the bus in time to see what had happened, so now all of them were in hysterics too – all of them, that is, except Mrs Milo, who was striding towards Anton with a *really* fierce look on her face.

Sanjeev rubbed the side of his head. It hurt! He was so busy rubbing his head and hoping Mrs Milo was going to bury Anton he didn't notice Jigsaw's favourite toy fall from his pocket and land on the snowy ground next to the woman's blanket.

One minute the toy was there; the next, it was gone.

After Mrs Milo had given Anton a tongue-lashing for throwing the snowball at Sanjeev and threatened to exclude him from any future trip if he gave her one more excuse, the smirk on Anton's face had slipped away.

When Mrs Milo finally turned away, Sanjeev shoved Anton. 'Idiot!' he snarled.

'Sorry, man,' said Anton, as they began the short walk from the bus to the station. 'Didn't mean to hurt you.'

But Sanjeev was too annoyed to let it go that easily. It wasn't until they got to the train that Anton realised Sanjeev was still angry. 'Okay, look, I'm sorry,' Anton said again and stuck out a hand. 'It was dumb. *I'm* dumb!'

Sanjeev looked into Anton's face and hesitated for a second. Then he shook Anton's hand.

'And I really do think your gloves are cool,' Anton said.

'Don't push it!' Sanjeev replied.

CHAPTER 19

—

The journey on the train from Hoboken to 33rd Street passed quickly. Sanjeev and Anton had watched the rest of *Forensics Five-O* while Jermaine and Basem had played *Breakneck* on Basem's mobile. When they arrived at 33rd Street, Mrs Milo rounded up the class, herding them onto the correct trains.

The first journey on the PATH train had been okay, but the last leg was making Sanjeev feel horrible. It felt as if the train were shrinking in size, that the ceiling was getting lower and lower, and the air inside the train thinner and thinner. As soon as the train pulled into 86th Street, there was only one thought in his mind: get onto the street. And that's what he did. Faster than any of his friends, he rushed to the top of the 86th Street exit stairs and stood there waiting, panting hard. How good it was to be outside again – even if the air was so cold it burned his lungs!

Class 8's laughs and the slap, slap, slap of their feet as they climbed the stairs echoed below. Down the street, an old woman walking a poodle caught Sanjeev's eye. The poodle wore a tartan coat that matched its little tartan hat and ridiculous tartan boots. He thought of Jigsaw in those boots. It almost made him laugh. He took a deep breath. The freezing air had burned his lungs, but he was feeling calmer now. He would have to return home by subway too though. He groaned and squeezed his eyes shut, trying to force the idea out of his brain.

'Hey, what's the big hurry?' Sanjeev turned and met Anton's questioning gaze.

He shrugged. 'Just felt like I had to get out.'

'You okay?' Anton asked.

'Sure,' Sanjeev said. Anton shrugged and the two boys took in the scene in front of them. With all the clothes they were wearing, the Upper East Side New Yorkers hurrying past looked twice the normal size of humans.

After a short walk, they finally arrived at the Metropolitan Museum of Art. As Class 8 stepped inside, a hushed 'Wow!' arose. They were standing in an enormous lobby that was called, according to Mrs Milo, the Great Hall. It wasn't hard to understand why. Sanjeev stared up at the ceiling. Broad stone arches, like stone waves, stretched and curved high above him, supporting a vast dome. At the centre of the dome, like a huge eye, there was a circular window through which daylight was falling. Sanjeev blinked. It felt as though the wide, blue eye was watching their every move…

'Right,' Mrs Milo said, 'the Silk Road exhibition is in Exhibition Gallery 899. Please stay together as we go there.' Mrs Milo's eyes stayed glued to Anton as she said this. 'Is everyone ready?'

There were nods all round.

'Right, let's go!' Mrs Milo said and led them into the museum.

One of the first galleries they walked through was full of European vases from the Castle of Vélez Blanco, then they went past the Thomas J Watson library and some huge bronze statues. Finally, they arrived at Exhibition Gallery 899. Mrs Milo spoke with a woman at the entry desk, while some of the class already moved through the turnstile and into the exhibition space. Sanjeev gazed behind the turnstile. The entire wall had been covered by a huge poster titled, *The Silk Road – a Journey in Time*. But that wasn't what had made Sanjeev's mouth fall open.

'Yo!' said Anton. 'Let's go.'

'Huh?' said Sanjeev.

'Let's go, dude. Time to journey in time!'

'Er... Okay,' said Sanjeev. But he didn't move. Instead, his eyes remained on the Silk Road poster. On it, there was a mosaic picture of a woman, her hair short and curled, with a sort of crown in it. Her mouth was small, her eyes big and staring.

Anton stopped and looked at his friend. Then he looked at the poster. 'Know her?' he asked, grinning.

'No, but I don't know, there's something about her that seems so familiar.'

'Maybe she's in one of your Mom's art books?'

'Yeah, that's probably it.'

CHAPTER 20

Inside the exhibition, the class gathered in a gallery so huge it almost stole Mrs Milo's voice as she spoke. Sanjeev looked around. Glass display cases lined the room in rows all the way up the middle towards another door and another room, like bones in a spinal column. The place was practically empty; two or three people stood at the far end, but that was all. Sanjeev guessed the weather had kept visitors away.

Sanjeev looked at the introduction to the exhibition on the wall. It was a huge graphic titled *A Multitude of Roads* and it traced the routes on a map by which goods travelled east to west and vice versa. It told Sanjeev something he already knew: there was no single Silk Road. With red lines it showed the Silk Road was actually many, many routes; Sanjeev was reminded of veins, veins that ran not just across continents, but seas too. With his eyes, he followed one route from Hangzhou on the edge of the East China Sea, through China, past the Jade Gates, around the Taklamakan Desert, into Kashgar, through the Pamir Mountains, past Samarkand, around the Caspian Sea, over the Caucasus Mountains, down to Antioch, and across to Byzantium, which lay at the mouth of the Black Sea. What an incredible journey. Sanjeev wondered how long it would have taken. Years, he supposed. And it wasn't just silk that travellers exchanged, there would have been cultural beliefs, technological advances, as well as all other sorts of goods. It was a network, much like the internet, only it was two thousand years old.

'Now take your time and read the information on the placards,' Mrs Milo was saying. 'Think about how the objects and pictures tell the story of the Silk Road.'

Sanjeev glanced sideways at Anton. One look at Anton's face was enough; Sanjeev knew Mrs Milo's wishes would not be granted anytime soon.

'When everyone's finished, we'll meet at the desk where I picked up the tickets. Is everyone clear?'

Everyone nodded their heads – except Anton, who was busy shooting meaningful looks at Jermaine and Basem. It didn't take a genius to work out they were planning something. Just in case there was any doubt, as soon as the group broke up, Jermaine and Basem huddled around Anton and Sanjeev.

'The sooner we get round these suckers,' Anton said, nodding to the priceless artefacts in the gallery, 'the sooner we get out.' Jermaine and Basem were nodding and smiling. Sanjeev must have looked puzzled. 'Cafe, dude,' said Anton. 'The cafe's right next to the Silk Road entrance.'

'The cafe?' said Sanjeev. 'What's so exciting about the cafe?'

'Absolutely nothing,' replied Anton, 'but it's way better than this place. Plus, I can play *Breakneck* without Mrs Milo seeing me!' He drew his mobile from his jacket pocket and waved it around.

'Yeah!' said Basem.

'Alright!' echoed Jermaine.

Sanjeev shook his head. What could he say?

'You coming?' asked Anton, half-turning away from Sanjeev as though he already knew the answer.

'You guys go ahead, I'll catch you up later.'

Anton shrugged and, followed by Jermaine and Basem, began zooming past all the exhibits. Sanjeev watched them go. He was annoyed. What was the point of coming all the way here if all you were going to do was play *Breakneck*?

Frowning, Sanjeev went and stood in front of the first display case. He looked in. Several white, oblong shapes caught his eye. Reading the placard next to them, he discovered that these were silkworm cocoons and inside each was the larva of the silk moth. According to the little placard, silkworms needed a lot of care: they only ate fresh mulberry bush leaves and required a constant temperature – too hot or too cold and they died. He also discovered that the larvae are boiled alive in their cocoons in order to unravel the silk.

He had read somewhere that some people outside of China thought silk grew on trees – maybe it was the Romans. Perhaps that wasn't so surprising: China, the first country to produce lots of silk, kept the silk-making process a secret.

He looked at another placard. It was next to a Roman clasp for a toga. Back then, the placard said, silk was a luxury fabric. Everyone wanted it. They even passed a law in Rome about who could and couldn't wear it. So out went the silk from China to the West, and back came tonnes and tonnes of gold and precious gems. Traders travelled thousands of miles, crossed deserts, mountains and seas – and all because of a little worm. Sanjeev shook his head. It was amazing when you thought about it.

He stepped towards the next glass display case, still reflecting on the impact that a worm had on world history when, all of a sudden, he felt like his legs were about to slide away from him, like he had just stepped on black ice. But not only did it seem like he was about to take a tumble, he also felt giddy, as if his stomach somersaulted. He staggered forward, hands out in front of him, and bumped up against the display case. Panicked, and holding on to the display case like it was a life raft, he looked around. Mrs Milo was deep in conversation with a few of his classmates; no one else was paying him any attention.

Sanjeev's breathing grew heavy. He had no idea why, but his heart beat erratically, thumping away in his ribcage like an angry bee trying to escape through a pane of glass. And not just that, but beads of sweat – sweat! – had formed on his brow. What was going on? Was he having a heart attack? Should he call out Mrs Milo's name? Did he need medical attention?

Racing thoughts fired through Sanjeev's brain, but his eyes hadn't moved. They were fixed on what was inside in the display case. Like limpets on a rock at the seashore, they were locked on, and barely registered the placard which read, *Lady with a cornucopia*. *Lady with a cornucopia*. The words ricocheted around his head.

What he saw was small and brown – part of a mosaic taken from somewhere in Constantinople. The two figures – one large, the other small – both formed more than 1,500 years ago using tiny pieces of coloured stone, stared back. The smaller figure was of a man wearing boots that reached up to his knees and a sort of dress. Maybe it was a toga. In his hand, he was carrying what looked like a huge cone, but instead of scoops of ice cream, there were flowers in it. He was holding it in both hands, bringing it towards the woman.

And then, somehow, he was falling into the mosaic itself: an endless, dark space with multi-coloured, kaleidoscopic mists like snakes' tongues that swirled and surged and licked towards him while thousands of brilliantly white objects flashed past like meteors.

He screamed at the top of his lungs, but nothing escaped his lips. Whether he was falling or rising, he had no idea. Weightless yet travelling, utterly terrified, he felt his body twist and turn, as helpless as a feather in a hurricane.

PART 5

BYZANTIUM ⚊ CIRCA 525 AD

Chapter 21

Whatever Sanjeev was lying on, he liked it: it was warm and comfy and gave him the feeling he had enjoyed a long, relaxing rest. His mind drifted a little, floating in a sort of sleepy, contented haze. Maybe he would snooze a little longer… But no sooner had he thought this when something rough and slimy dragged itself across his face, cheek to cheek. It felt like a big, wet towel. *Jigsaw's licking my face!*

Sanjeev opened his eyes. Two great, hairy nostrils floated centimetres from his face. Beyond the nostrils, a pair of dark eyes fluttered behind long eyelashes. Stunned, Sanjeev stared up at the beast looking down at him, its face covered in tawny fur, its lower jaw rolling from side to side. Suddenly, from between its yellow teeth, a monstrous tongue emerged and began to stretch out…

'Arrrrgh!' Sanjeev yelled, his scream partly muffled as he rolled face-first into sand. Jumping to his feet and wiping the sand from his eyes, he stared at the beast, which craned its long neck towards him as a wave of musky smell wafted his way. He was staring at a camel. Four camels, in fact. On their two-humped backs were woven saddlebags covered with intricate geometric patterns. Gourds and bags, tied tight with brightly-coloured ropes and ribbons, hung from large wooden saddles.

'What the…?' he shouted, trying to take in the scene in front of him. Beside the camels was… His brain refused to conjure the word. Tall trees swayed, a bird fluttered from one branch to another, a red ball of fire sank further towards a distant mountain range in the west. A LAKE! He was standing looking at a group of four camels under the shade of slender trees that clustered around a lake!

This was not the Met – not unless they had introduced the best ever 3D interactive display. It wasn't New Jersey, and it wasn't anywhere he had ever seen in his life before. Oh, no! Yet another wild, imaginative journey?

The camel that had licked him was still staring at him.

'Where am I?' he shouted at it, as he suppressed a rising sense of panic. His mindfulness class at school was finally becoming useful, and he instinctively knew losing his cool would not help. He slowly raised both his hands to his eyes, touching his closed eyelids. No glasses, and yet when he opened his eyes he could see perfectly. He relaxed. Clearly this was a truly surreal dream. He needed to go with the flow on this one. The hallucination seemed so real, and his breathing steadied as he looked around.

Suddenly, there was movement. His heart jumped into his throat. He wasn't alone. Through the trees, he caught a glimpse of three men on the far side of the pool, walking slowly towards him. Sanjeev instinctively swerved past the camels and ran behind the nearest tree. He poked his head around the trunk. All three men had dark beards and were wearing loose dark brown robes tied at the waist. The nearest was a squat man with broad shoulders and a fierce face. His eyes were so close together, he almost looked like he was watching his own nose. The next was the tallest and thinnest, and was grinning. The other man, the shortest of the three, and much shorter than Sanjeev, was walking with a crutch.

'Hey, Boy!' the man with the crutch called. 'Get those camels hobbled and tethered. How many times do I have to tell you?'

Like a startled tortoise, Sanjeev pulled his head out of sight. *There's a fourth person here,* he thought, frantically scouring the immediate area but seeing nothing except trees and camels. But wait. Where was the fourth person? Sanjeev scanned the trees but saw no one else.

He took a deep breath. Slowly, he poked his head around the trunk again.

The man with the fierce face was stomping past the nearest edge of the water and heading straight for the tree where Sanjeev was trying to hide. *Think of something!* Sanjeev told himself. A second ticked by, then another and another. He stood, frozen to the spot.

And then the man was there, standing in front of him, eyes blazing, huge beard bristling. Sanjeev held his breath while his heart thudded against this chest wall. And waited – waited for the man to pull out a huge hunting knife and cut him up there and then like a chicken fillet.

'If you want something done, do it yourself,' the man shouted, then added, 'Get our grub out of the bags while I hobble and tether the camels.'

Sanjeev stared mutely at the man. The man returned Sanjeev's stare. 'Well?' the man yelled. 'What are you waiting for boy? If you don't want a clout on the ear, you better get a move on!'

For a moment, the man stood staring at him in silence. Then he clicked his fingers in front of Sanjeev's face. 'Hey! Is there anyone in there? Go and get the food – now!'

'Food, now,' Sanjeev said in a robotic voice, but even as he said it, he realised he wasn't speaking English…

The man's eyes narrowed, and he shook his head. 'I swear, when we get to Byzantium, we are going to sell you.'

Sanjeev was too afraid to speak. This hallucination was too real for his liking. How could he end it? Should he pinch himself or smack his head? Had he fallen asleep on the school trip? Was he in sickbay at the Met? Until he snapped out of this, he'd have to do whatever these people wanted him to.

CHAPTER 22

—

Sanjeev watched the stars above flicker and burn while the camels made sleepy grunts, the fire crackled and the three men snored. Sanjeev had never slept like this – with no roof above him, and with no lights from cars or houses. It was the darkest dark he had ever seen, broken only by the glorious stretch of the Milky Way above him. It was so low he could almost touch it – and he finally understood why the Romans had first called it the *via lacteal* – the road of milk. It was quite magical.

Sanjeev's stomach rumbled. He was confused, exhausted and ravenous. Dinner had been a few dried biscuits and some dates. Almost as soon as they had finished eating it, the men had unpacked their blankets and slept, but not before the one with the beard had warned Sanjeev to wake up early and feed the camels – or else. Sanjeev wondered how he could do that without his alarm clock, but he'd cross that bridge when he came to it. Perhaps his alarm clock would materialise in this strange experience? Freud would have a wonderful time with him on the couch.

Although he knew deep down that this was not reality, still Sanjeev thought about his three imaginary travelling companions. He had learned all their names, and the one called Brother Thomas, the one with the thickest beard, was the most terrifying. Behind that beard, Brother Thomas's eyes darted like cobras, and he always seemed on the verge of losing his temper. Brother Luke, taller and leaner than the others, was much calmer. He grinned a lot of the time, not caring that he lacked two front teeth. Brother Mark, the shortest of the three, had huge ears out of which black hair sprouted like some dark creature's claws. Brother Mark always carried a long, wooden crutch, of which he never let go. All three brothers wore a single piece of woolly, brown cloth. Armless and stretching to the knee, the cloth collected at the waist by a thick leather belt.

As he lay staring at the stars above him, Sanjeev thought about all that had happened in the last few hours. The facts seemed simple enough. One minute he had been in the Met museum, about to enjoy an exhibition on the Silk Road; the next, he was in the middle of nowhere travelling with three monks who were returning to Byzantium. The brothers didn't know his name and insisted on calling him 'Boy', but they also thought he had travelled with them since India, which they had passed through on the first leg of their journey. From what Sanjeev could figure out, they had been as far as China, and were now at the edge of the Taklamakan Desert, heading west, on their way back to Byzantium. After the Taklamakan Desert, the quickest route back to Byzantium was through the territory of the Sasanian Empire, but for some reason, the Sasanians scared the brothers. He had no idea why.

Also incredibly puzzling was his sudden ability to jabber away in a language he knew wasn't English or Bengali. If the brothers were from Byzantium, they were probably speaking ancient Greek… which meant that *he* might be speaking ancient Greek! He scratched at the woollen *things* he was wearing. Definitely *not* what he'd worn to the Met! The torn tunic and undergarments smelled like they were made of camel dung, which was bewildering *and* disgusting. If this were an alternative reality he'd somehow been thrown into, it seemed way too smelly, itchy, and… freaky for comfort.

Then there were the brothers. Something was *definitely* not right about them. They were on tenterhooks the whole time, startling at the smallest sound, scanning the horizon, and generally being afraid of their shadows. And then there was the campfire. When he'd suggested making one, the three brothers had called him all sorts of names and Brother Thomas had even cuffed his ear, telling him he was the dumbest creature in all creation and that the smoke from a fire would be seen from here to Antioch. But so what if someone saw the fire? Why were they so worried about their location being known?

Still staring up at the night sky, Sanjeev found the guardians of the pole and traced a line from them to Polaris – the North Pole star, the point around which the heavens seemed to turn as though it were the centre of the universe. Sanjeev couldn't explain it, but seeing Polaris was a comfort. Was it because he had gazed up at the night sky so many times from his bedroom in New Jersey?

He swallowed hard. New Jersey. His bedroom. His parents. Jigsaw. He shook his head. Getting upset wasn't going to help. He had to reason things out. If this was some sort of dream, he told himself, he would have to wait until he was ready to wake up. But then he thought about *Planet Odyssey*, and an episode called "*Yesterday is Tomorrow*". In it, *Endeavour* and its crew travelled back in time to Earth in the 1980s. Was that it? Had he entered some kind of time warp? Had he somehow been transported back in time? If that was true, how had it happened? In that episode, the *Endeavour* had entered a black hole – but all he had done was go to the Met! If it was a dream, how come his ear still hurt and felt extra warm from the cuffing that Brother Thomas gave it? Could he be stuck here forever in a kind of mental paralysis? *If I can feel pain and wasn't dreaming, could I... die here?*

The foot that struck his ribs struck again.

'Hey!' yelled Sanjeev, opening his eyes, then shutting them again as bright light flooded in.

'Get up!' Brother Thomas yelled. 'Didn't I tell you to feed the camels?' He pulled his foot all the way back to deliver a really meaty kick.

His eyes suddenly flicked wide open, and Sanjeev rolled. Brother Thomas swung – and missed. The momentum of the kick lifted Brother Thomas off his feet and into the air, a startled look on his face. Then gravity intervened. Brother Thomas landed on his back, legs and arms akimbo. A cloud of dust rose. 'Why you little…!' he groaned. While getting to his feet, he spotted a stick. His eyes brightened. He snatched it up and lunged at Sanjeev, lashing the stick back and forth like a whip. But Sanjeev was too quick. He took off like a scalded cat. Brother Thomas rushed after him while Brother Mark and Luke roared with laughter.

'Run, Boy, run!' shouted Brother Luke, laughing, 'Or surely Brother Thomas will murder you.'

'Come, Brother Thomas,' cried Brother Mark. 'Can you not catch such a small mouse? Truly you are getting old.'

Brother Thomas, face the colour of molten lava, redoubled his efforts. But Sanjeev was too fast. Ducking and diving, he dodged every blow. After several minutes, Brother Thomas staggered to a halt. Chest heaving, he threw down the stick and stamped on it as though it was on fire. Brother Mark, hobbling on his crutch and trying not to laugh, came and put an arm around Brother Thomas's shoulder. 'Come, Brother Thomas,' said Brother Mark soothingly. 'Remember: a stone is heavy and the sand weighty, but the provocation of a fool is heavier than both.'

Secretly, Brother Mark winked at Sanjeev, who was standing a few metres away. Brother Mark motioned with his head for Sanjeev to go and attend to the camels as he led Brother Thomas back to the camp.

Sanjeev, careful to remain outside the range of a kick from Brother Thomas, walked over to the camels and began feeding them.

So much for keeping my head down, he thought miserably. He wondered whether he would even remember this nightmare once he woke up.

CHAPTER 23

—

Breakfast had been more dried dates that Sanjeev was already beginning to hate, and their bed blankets were rolled, packed into bags, and lashed onto the camels. There was just one more thing to do: Sanjeev had to get on his camel. He stared at the animal. It was the one who had licked his face. He could see that behind her long eyelashes, her big, brown eyes were watching him. He had never seen a real camel before, never mind ridden on one. Was it camels or llamas that spat? He wasn't sure. So far, at least, she hadn't done that. But how would she react when he tried to get on the saddle strapped between her two humps? He had a vision of Daisy – he had decided to call her that – throwing him off like a bucking bronco.

'Get a move on,' yelled Brother Thomas, who was already on his camel. 'We want to make Kashgar soon.'

Sanjeev ran his hand through his hair. He had hoped he would fall asleep under the stars and wake up in his own bed in New Jersey. But instead of the birds chirping on his mobile, Brother Thomas's foot in his ribs had been his wake-up call. He sighed.

Daisy turned and looked at him. She was sitting with her four legs folded under her large body. He gathered up her reins, just as the brothers had done. 'I'm gonna get on now,' he said, pulling himself up towards the funny-shaped saddle. Daisy continued to chew. Sanjeev slowly sat down, a rein in each hand, legs splayed across Daisy's broad back. He squeezed his legs together as best he could, trying to grip Daisy's bony flesh. He rapped the saddle and confirmed it was made of rock-hard wood, but at least there were thick blankets laid across the saddle. Could he really survive a long journey on this? He looked up. Brother Thomas, Luke and Mark, whose camels were in front of him, had turned around and were staring at him. Sanjeev gave a sheepish grin and straightened up. Brother Thomas spat noisily. The camels on which the three brothers sat started to plod forward.

Sanjeev took a deep breath. He'd never ridden a horse before, let alone a camel. How did you get one to start? Was there a special word? He hadn't heard the brothers say anything to their camels, but perhaps he'd missed it. He searched his memory for something appropriate. Nothing came to mind. He shrugged. 'Go!' he cried. 'Come on! Go!'

The words were barely out of his mouth when his whole world lurched violently to the left, almost flinging him to the ground. A moment later, it lurched again, and he was propelled in the opposite direction. Daisy lurched for a third time, then Sanjeev had the sensation of being raised up in the air by a very slow lift. He opened his eyes and looked down. He was now nestled safely between two hairy humps two metres off the ground.

With Brother Mark at the front, followed by Brother Thomas and Brother Luke, Sanjeev and Daisy followed at the rear. Although it was early morning, the sun was beginning to warm the air, shining brightly through the trees and making Sanjeev squint. As Daisy plodded along, Sanjeev was tipped to one side then the other, over and over again. Before long, his backside was aching and he was ready to jump off. But he knew he couldn't. If he did, Brother Thomas would go mad. He focused on the track ahead, which was just a sandy trail. He had to get through this.

To take his attention away from the pain, Sanjeev tried to think of all the food he was going to eat when he got back home – and he had decided he was going to get home. He really missed his mum's spicy omelet. She made it with tomatoes, onions, coriander and chillis and they had it pretty much every weekend. But the pain was impossible to ignore. How did the brothers do it? How did they manage to sit on the wooden saddle for so long? Then it occurred to Sanjeev that he had probably been in the wooden saddle for less than twenty minutes.

Nine days later, Sanjeev had been sitting on the wooden saddle for more hours than he could count. Kashgar had come and gone. A dusty, bustling town, they had picked up supplies there – more dried dates, more dried apricots – and carried on, with Brother Thomas warning Sanjeev not to discuss their business with anyone. *What a joke*: only the monks knew the truth. And they weren't telling anyone. He'd tried to get some information about why they had travelled so far. But each time he was either ignored or told to shut up.

During those nine days, the distant mountains beyond Kashgar had inched closer. At first, they had appeared on the horizon as shimmering mirages above the hot, dusty sands around them. Then, their liquid, wavering forms had become more solid, more real. Soon, individual peaks had appeared. And as the sands around the four of them had given way to grasslands and they had continued past Kashgar towards Panjikent, so the mountains had continued to grow and grow, until they had become impossibly stern and unapproachable guardians of the lands beyond. Sanjeev had hoped with all his might that the brothers really did know how to thread their way through such giants because there was no way he was going to be able to climb even the smallest of them.

Two mornings after they entered the Pamir Mountains, Sanjeev, shivering in the cold air, woke early, fed the camels, cleaned up the campsite, and rolled and packed the blankets. It was the same routine over and over again and he was beginning to feel like a character in one of his father's favourite movies, *Groundhog Day*!

'Let's go!' Brother Mark called when everything was packed.

When Sanjeev got on Daisy, it suddenly dawned on him that he was getting used to the saddle. He was actually able to sit on the wooden thing without cringing.

As the caravan moved across the rocky ground towards a distant ravine, Sanjeev stared at Brother Mark who was at the front.

Last night, when he thought everyone else was asleep, he'd witnessed something really strange. Lying in the darkness, thinking about his mum, dad, Jigsaw, he had felt really blue. He was really missing them. And what must they be thinking? Had they called the police? Was there a nationwide hunt on to find him? His mind racing, he'd lain thinking about home for ages. Just when he had finally felt sleepy, a shadowy figure had stumbled past him, clutching his stomach and heading for some nearby bushes. 'Good luck finding toilet paper,' thought Sanjeev and he was closing his eyes again when he suddenly realised who had passed by. He sat bolt upright and stared into the moonless night as the figure disappeared. *It couldn't have been, could it?* He had lain back down, but the thought had stayed with him. Brother Mark had walked past him and he hadn't been carrying his crutch! Even though Sanjeev had practically held his eyelids open, waiting for another glimpse of Brother Mark, he had fallen asleep.

Sanjeev continued to stare at Brother Mark and his crutch, which was pushed into a kind of sling that hung from the saddle.

What was the point of pretending you needed a crutch? Sanjeev wondered. Instead of trying to figure that one out, for the millionth time he thought about how he had got from the Met in New York to the middle of the Pamir Mountains. It was a mind-boggler. There were way too many unknowns – way too many variables whose values needed to be established, as his science teacher, Mrs Fernandez liked to say. Mrs Fernandez also liked to say that a big part of being a good scientist was having a good imagination. Einstein had had a good imagination – look at all the thought experiments he'd done – but Sanjeev felt even Einstein would have had trouble working out what was going on here!

The days wore on. Perched on Daisy, jostled from side to side as the hard little seat rolled back and forth, they followed the rocky brown path as it slipped between the massive peaks and sharp ridges all around them.

On their sixth day in the mountains, their path took them through a forest. They were now bathed in shades of green. An hour or so later, they stood on the edge of a sheer drop. A huge, broad valley stretched far into the distance. The valley was flanked by rocky foothills, which climbed up towards mountains with sharp, snow-tipped peaks. A thin haze hung over the valley floor, and a river swerved through it, a dark, tangled ribbon. On either side of the river, fields of every shade of green made the valley look like a huge, patchwork quilt. Sanjeev imagined bent-back farmers busy working the soil, but he couldn't see anyone – probably too far away. He turned and looked behind. Other mountain peaks loomed, stern giants staring in stony silence. He hadn't realised they had camped so high up. *No wonder I was freezing last night,* he thought. To his left, the forest they were journeying through continued all the way down the mountain, its trees getting smaller and smaller until, at the bottom, they looked as tiny as the hairs on his arm.

'Well?' Brother Thomas said, swivelling in his saddle and directing an angry look at Sanjeev.

'Er... well, what?' Sanjeev asked.

'What are you waiting for?'

'Pull her to the left!' Brother Thomas shouted. 'There's more space.'

Sanjeev pulled. Daisy trudged forward. Sanjeev heaved on the reins, pulling with all his might. Lingering over the void, Daisy's head swung left, then slowly her whole body turned. Sanjeev glanced under his arm and gulped. The edge was two metres away. A stone, kicked by Daisy, rolled over, disappearing in an instant. Daisy continued to turn. Sanjeev let out a big sigh of relief. She had turned all the way around and was heading back into the forest. As soon as he was safely amongst the trees again, Sanjeev watched as the three brothers turned their camels around and came clomping back after they had seen all they wanted of the view. Brother Thomas was opening his mouth to say something – something nasty, Sanjeev was sure – when a shout made all of them jump.

'Make way!' a voice cried, and a moment later a horse and its rider galloped past them. They watched in astonishment as the rider and his horse disappeared amongst the trees and the gloom.

In unison, Brother Thomas and Brother Luke leaped off their camels and ran to Brother Mark. All three began talking in whispers and pointing to where the rider – a messenger, perhaps – had disappeared. Brother Thomas's eyes were like a couple of saucers staring out of his face, Brother Mark was curled over his crutch as though someone had punched him in the stomach, and Brother Luke was twitching and fidgeting like a leaf on a windy day.

As they continued, Sanjeev grew more and more curious. If only he could get a little closer… He was slipping one leg off the saddle when the brothers turned. In a flash, he regained the saddle, watching as the brothers came running back and clambered onto their camels. A moment later, they were on the move again, but with an urgency that had doubled the pace.

Whatever it was, they obviously weren't going to tell him. And whatever it was, it had seriously spooked the brothers.

CHAPTER 24

—

Many hours passed before they saw the rider again. How late in the day it was, Sanjeev had no idea, but the air had cooled, the sun had fallen low on the horizon, and darkness had crept out of its lair. They had found a path and climbed down the mountainside, entering the last of the forest as the landscape flattened out. At first glance, Sanjeev had thought it was a pile of stones, or perhaps an animal resting beneath the broad canopy of an oak tree that stood on the edge of the forest next to meadows and fields of lumpen earth. As they drew nearer, Brother Mark began turning around and casting looks at Luke and Thomas. Sanjeev was puzzled by Brother Mark's expression – a mix of bafflement and something else. Moving even closer to the tree, Sanjeev gasped.

A dead man was lying under the oak, both legs straight, his arm curled around his head. And in the meadow next to the river, grazing on the lush grass, was the dead man's horse. The same one that had passed them earlier in the forest.

Sanjeev's stomach heaved and his head swam as he gazed at the corpse. This wasn't like *Forensics Five-O*. The expression on the man's paper-white face was horrible: a twisted, surprised look. Real blood, heavy and dark, was soaking into the dry leaves around him and flies were buzzing around the wound in his neck and little insects were crawling around the wound.

Someone had murdered the man. Despite all the killings he had seen on TV shows, Sanjeev had never given them a second thought:

all those TV deaths – thousands of them, perhaps – hadn't seemed real. But this… this was different. He didn't know if he had travelled through time and space, didn't know if he had entered some kind of alternate reality. But whatever had happened, he knew one thing for sure: it felt very, very real. It felt like a person had died. Sanjeev felt a sudden deep sadness for this man he didn't know. He likely had a family, maybe even children, who would now not see him alive again.

Daisy halted behind Brother Mark's camel. Brother Thomas gave Sanjeev a stay-where-you-are look and ran with Brother Luke towards Brother Mark, who had already got off his camel and was walking towards the body.

They gathered around the man's unnaturally still body for a moment, but instead of examining it closely, the three brothers began scouring the ground, looking for something. As they kicked at dead leaves, they circled and re-circled the oak; then they regrouped and began arguing in furious, hushed voices.

Now what are they up to? Sanjeev was wondering when Brother Mark let out a terrified gasp. He pointed down the valley. Sanjeev followed his finger.

Amongst the lengthening and deepening shadows, a dust cloud was rising.

'Soldiers!' Brother Thomas said. 'We have to run.'

'What?' shouted Brother Luke. 'No! If we run, we'll look guilty.' He grabbed Brother Thomas by the arm. 'We have to stay here. Don't you understand that?'

Brother Thomas, furious at being spoken to so roughly, tried to push Brother Luke away. As they struggled, they slipped; both lost their balance and toppled over, but they continued to grapple. Brother Mark, not sure which side to take, was trying to pull them apart, hopping on his crutch, telling them to calm down and think.

'Stop it, you fools, or you'll get us all hanged,' he was yelling. As the word 'hanged' rang in Sanjeev's ears, Brother Thomas and Brother Luke suddenly stopped fighting and stared into the distance. And now Sanjeev saw it too: an approaching dust cloud; and felt it: the vibrations of many hooves furiously pounding the earth.

By the time the detachment of soldiers arrived, the brothers had dusted off their clothes and were standing side by side, eyes wide with fear. Sanjeev realised they had been lucky: the ridiculous scuffle had taken place behind the oak's wide trunk; the soldiers wouldn't have seen a thing. However, as soon as the riders entered the edge of the forest, they saw the dead body.

The captain, pulling on his reins, looked at Sanjeev, who was still on Daisy. 'Join your friends,' he called. The words sounded different to those the brothers had been using; nevertheless, Sanjeev understood. Could he now understand every language there was in this alternate reality? Was he now super-multilingual? How cool would that—

'Move!' the captain cried.

Sanjeev did as he was told.

The soldiers, about twenty of them, formed a circle around the three brothers and Sanjeev. Sanjeev looked up at the captain, who was riding a small, light brown horse. Although the captain had a big belly and an untidy beard, he was sitting very upright on his horse and his eyes were as dark and hard as two pebbles in a river. 'You four,' the captain said coldly, 'are under arrest.'

CHAPTER 25

—

One of the soldiers wrapped a rope around Sanjeev's wrists behind his back, tied two knots and pushed him down on his knees next to the others. Brother Mark's crutch lay next to him, and Brother Thomas and Brother Luke's eyes, Sanjeev noticed, seemed glued to it.

The soldier snapped to attention. 'Prisoners secured, sir,' he said. The captain nodded. The soldier saluted, ran to his horse, and stood by it.

Sanjeev concentrated on keeping his breathing even and calm, but his heart was hammering like crazy.

The captain dismounted smartly from his horse, walked to the tree, swung his sword to the side, knelt, and began examining the dead man more closely. The other soldiers stood beside their horses, awaiting further orders.

After a few moments, the captain raised his head and spoke. 'His throat has been cut,' he said, addressing the man standing nearest him, who was tall and lean and had eyebrows that looked like two knife blades. 'Something – a necklace of some sort, perhaps – has been stolen from around his neck,' continued the captain, holding up two short pieces of leather. 'The murderer snapped the leather when he stole the object that was on it – a precious stone, or perhaps gold or silver. Certainly something valuable.' The captain shook his head sadly. 'A man's life for what? A piece of gold? Some money?'

Still kneeling, the captain lifted the dead man's torso slightly. The captain frowned and, standing up, he walked around the tree, keeping his eyes trained on the ground. A few steps later, he picked up what to Sanjeev looked like a small piece of paper. 'How was he riding?' he looked over at Sanjeev and the brothers.

The three brothers looked at one another, blank expressions on their faces. It was Sanjeev who eventually answered. 'When we saw him go past us earlier, he was galloping – going really fast. But I think he must have been resting here.'

The captain nodded and began mumbling almost to himself. 'By his uniform and this piece of scroll, he was obviously a messenger. He rode past the boy and his companions at a gallop, which implies he had news to take to the next town. So where are the rest of the scrolls he must have been carrying? Where is his bag?' With the piece of scroll still in his hand, he barked at the man with the sharp eyebrows. 'Lieutenant Han, I want an eight-man party. You are to look for a leather bag about this big,' he said, outlining the shape of a rectangle with his hands.

'Yes, sir,' replied Lieutenant Han. Yelling at eight of the soldiers, the lieutenant formed them into a little square. On his order, two soldiers each began moving east, west, north and south, eyes on the ground.

The captain watched them move out, then he turned to Sanjeev and smiled thinly. 'Right now, you are the only suspects we have. The punishment for murder, as you know, is death.'

The captain's words hit Sanjeev like a punch in the stomach. He glanced at the three brothers, their faces were trembling and pale with terror. Sanjeev took a deep breath.

'There has to be a motive,' he said, projecting his voice as confidently as he could – though his stomach was doing somersaults – 'and a means.'

The captain paid no attention. He was still watching his men as they spread out, tracing the cardinal points.

'There has to be a motive and a means,' Sanjeev repeated more loudly.

This time, the captain turned and stared. 'Who gave you permission to speak?'

Sanjeev bowed. 'I'm sorry. It's just—'

'Just what?' snapped the captain.

'There has to be a means. If the motive was to kill and steal, what did the murderer use to kill the messenger?'

'That,' the captain sneered, 'is rather obvious, isn't it?'

'A slit throat does suggest a knife,' replied Sanjeev, 'but look where we are.'

'What are you taking about?' yelled Brother Thomas, suddenly furious.

'Be quiet,' shouted the captain. 'Continue,' he said to Sanjeev.

'No one passed us on the road. And you, captain, passed no one?' The captain gave the slightest of nods. 'It means,' continued Sanjeev, 'that the murderer was already here when the messenger arrived. The murderer is probably one of the local farmers. He could have used a knife. But anything with a blade would have worked.'

CHAPTER 26

The captain's silence was making Sanjeev nervous. Even so, he knew his reasoning was sound. 'If the murderer is a farmer – who cut the messenger's throat in order to steal something valuable – then the murderer probably used something he carried with him every day, like a tool of some kind.' Sanjeev thought on his feet. 'I think the murderer still has the murder weapon... because a poor farmer wouldn't throw away a valuable tool. So, finding the weapon means finding the murderer.'

There was another long silence. Finally, the captain spoke. 'What makes you so sure the weapon isn't a knife?'

'I'm not sure it isn't, but if you look at the tools the farmers are using here, we'll find what the murderer used.'

The captain, Sanjeev, and the three brothers gazed through the trees and into the fields. 'Hmmm. I see what you mean,' the captain said, stroking his beard. 'It's not impossible. Alright, let's imagine you are correct. How can the actual murder weapon be found?'

'We'll do exactly what Song Ci did!' Sanjeev answered.

'Song Ci? Who's he? I've never heard of him.'

'He's a...' Sanjeev said, but stopped. He realised that Song Ci may not have even been born yet, but that didn't matter for his purposes. The idea for what he was planning had come from a *Forensics Five-O* episode in which police Captain Max Eastern had mentioned Song Ci to one of the show's other detectives. After the episode finished, Sanjeev had Googled the name.

Song Ci, he discovered, was a famous 13th Century Chinese coroner who used his knowledge of nature to solve murders. His book, *The Washing Away of Wrongs*, was used for hundreds of years in China in criminal investigations. Sanjeev took a deep breath. 'Song Ci was a famous master from Hunan province. He was a genius, but not everyone liked his ideas. In fact, only the smartest officials supported him. You see, Song Ci used strange methods to solve the crimes he investigated. But his methods worked, and that's the point, right? He always caught the real criminal – never took the easy way out, never arrested a scapegoat.'

The captain's eyes narrowed. 'So, you think you are scapegoats?'

'I understand why you arrested us,' replied Sanjeev carefully. 'But I can prove we didn't kill the messenger. And I think you are more interested in justice than the appearance of justice.' Sanjeev swallowed – his throat tightened. He imagined the thick strands of a noose slipping over his neck...

Time froze. The breeze died. Apart from Brother Thomas's pathetic sobs, silence fell.

'Very well,' the captain said after a pause that seemed to last two lifetimes. 'What do you suggest?'

'If you send out some of your men,' Sanjeev said, pointing to the soldiers who remained, 'they could find all the farmers in the area and bring them here. And the farmers could be told to bring everything they have with them in the fields... If you think that's a good idea.'

With no hesitation, the captain snapped his head around and barked out the order. 'Do it!' he commanded. 'Go to the nearest fields. Bring the farmers.'

Immediately, the remaining soldiers dispersed, galloping out of the woods. The captain turned, marched over to Sanjeev and stood beside him. 'Stand up,' he ordered. Sanjeev stood. 'Now quietly tell me your plan.'

When Sanjeev was finished, the captain thought for a moment and spoke. 'I hope for your sake it works.'

All six of the farmers gathered from the fields were sitting in a semi-circle in front of the captain and Sanjeev, heads bowed, shoulders hunched, their tanned faces shaded beneath their broad hats. Their long shadows extending out into the fields.

Lying on the ground in front of each man was a hand scythe.

'Cover your scythe with a cloth for the moment!' The men scrambled, some tearing a little of their tunics to cover the blades. 'You all know that a short while ago a man was murdered,' the captain said, pointing to the body that had been wrapped in a blanket and was being taken out of the forest on the back of a horse. 'None of you saw anything, you have already told us that. Take everything out of your pockets and place it on the ground in front of you. Do it now.'

Without a grumble, out came some dried biscuits, seeds, and some pieces of rope. All were laid carefully next to the scythes. On the captain's command, the soldiers began searching the farmers. When nothing else was found, the soldiers re-took their positions.

The second search party, sent out after the first, had orders to look for anything unusual. It didn't take them long to discover something.

'Sir,' one of the soldiers from the second party said, riding into the forest, 'I think we have found something of interest.'

'Follow me,' the captain ordered. Sanjeev walked behind the captain and the other soldier as they left the forest and entered the first field. Sanjeev could see that it was fallow. Dry grass grew in uneven clumps and loose stones were piled in small heaps at regular intervals across it. Near a huge boulder in the middle of the field, another soldier was standing and pointing at the ground. As they approached him, they could see a mound of newly disturbed soil. On top of the little mound sat a pale, very clean, rock.

'A marker,' Sanjeev said, staring at the stone.

The captain bent down, pushed the stone aside and dug into the earth with his fingers. He pulled some objects out of the soil. Between his hands, he rolled the objects a few times to clear away the dirt and then showed them to the soldiers and Sanjeev.

On the captain's palm were six large gold coins, but it was a small, stumpy key next to these that caught Sanjeev's eye. A monkey's face stared back at him, a smile bending the corners of its mouth. The expression was happy, maybe even kind of smug – as though it had gobbled down a load of bananas all by itself. The monkey's eyes were big and round, its ears also enormous, like the handles of a jug. As Sanjeev stared, the gold eyes blinked and the hair on the monkey's cheeks moved in the breeze. 'Did you see that?'

'See what?' the captain and his soldiers were looking curiously at Sanjeev.

'Ah, nothing, nothing at all,' spluttered Sanjeev.

'May I hold the key?' Sanjeev asked. The captain grunted and ordered a soldier to untie Sanjeev's ropes. The captain placed the key in Sanjeev's outstretched hand.

Although it was small, it was surprisingly heavy. *Solid gold*, thought Sanjeev. He turned it. He felt something other than weight in his hands, the key was vibrating and the gold was glinting and glowing brighter. The key was also getting heavier. The monkey's ears were wiggling and the hair on his cheeks and head were definitely moving in the breeze. Sanjeev looked round at everyone as they stared at him. No one else seemed to see anything different in the key! They were looking at him and not the key.

'A gold monkey key… but what does it open?' Sanjeev asked.

He fought an all-powerful impulse to put the key in his pocket and run for it. He'd never stolen anything in his life yet, but something about that key was drawing him in to forget about all potential danger. The soldiers were standing to one side of him now, opposite the captain. Could he barge through? How far could he get? 'It's so heavy for a such a little key,' he babbled. His hand began to close over the key slowly, his breathing a little heavier.

'Perhaps it was just the gold in it that the murderer wanted,' the captain said, pocketing, Sanjeev noticed, the six coins. 'These are very poor men. Even the small amount of gold in the key is more than they could hope to earn in a year.' The captain extended his hand to Sanjeev. The key got even heavier in Sanjeev's hand, but against all his deepest instincts, his hand shaking, he handed it back to the captain and watched as it joined the coins in his inner pocket. Without the key, Sanjeev was drained. His shoulders slumped, his feet lead, he followed the captain back.

Chapter 27

—

'Stand up, all of you. On your feet,' shouted the captain as he strode back into the forest.

Everyone – the six farmers and three brothers – jumped to their feet.

In his hands, the captain was holding three short knives he had taken from the three brother's saddlebags. 'Are these your knives?' he asked. The brothers agreed they were. 'Whose knife is this?'

'It's mine,' replied Brother Thomas.

The captain placed it at Brother Thomas's feet.

'And this?'

'Mine, sir,' said Brother Luke.

The captain placed it at Brother Luke's feet and put the last knife in front of Brother Mark.

'Do you all swear that these are your knives and they are the only knives you are carrying?'

'We do,' replied the brothers, looking puzzled and scared.

The captain turned to the farmers. 'Who was working in the fallow field today?'

For a moment, no one spoke. Then the tallest of the six farmers answered, head bowed. 'Sir, we all were. We took turns at collecting stones there. Didn't we?'

The five other farmers nodded.

'I see,' replied the captain. 'Each of you has a scythe,' said the captain. 'You are farmers, so you know your scythes very well.

Uncover the scythe in front of you now. Is your scythe the one in front of you or not? Look at it carefully and put it back down.'

The farmers picked up their scythes and began examining them, turning them over in their hands and touching the hooked blades. As Sanjeev watched, one of the farmers made eye contact, his small eyes locking onto Sanjeev's then shooting away again. Although all the farmers had beards, this particular man's was longer – it almost touched his chest. The farmers were laying down their scythes. The man with the long beard laid his down too.

'I want all of you to swear the scythe in front of you is your scythe and not someone else's. Do you swear?'

One by one, each farmer repeated the words, 'I swear.'

The farmer with the long beard was staring straight ahead, unblinking. The tallest farmer was frowning, puzzled but too scared to say anything. Brother Thomas's eyes were darting everywhere.

And just when Sanjeev was about to panic, the first one arrived.

CHAPTER 28

━

It appeared from nowhere, a fat, shiny, green metallic body bobbing in the air, darting here and there, slowing down and then speeding up. Twice it seemed like it was going to fly away, but then it made up its mind and came closer. Gold key forgotten, Sanjeev's heart was in his mouth. If this didn't work… He glanced at the captain. He was following it too.

Sanjeev's eyes turned in circles as he followed the fly's looping flight. Round and round and up and down it went: it flew between Brother Thomas and Brother Luke; it swerved around Brother Mark; it thought about landing on his crutch and shot up towards Brother Thomas's ear.

'Hands by your sides!' shouted the captain as Brother Thomas tried to shoo the fly away.

The fly flew on, zigging and zagging behind the six farmers, but with each zig and each zag, it seemed to be slowing down.

It's going to land, thought Sanjeev. But as soon as he thought this, the fly changed its mind and rose higher into the air. Sanjeev strained his eyes, but its shape and movement were lost in the shadows.

'Where…?'

'There!' The captain pointed.

Sanjeev lowered his gaze. The fly – was it the same one? – was circling the farmer who stood at the end of the row, a small man with a sharp face. Sanjeev could hear the fly's low, lazy buzz. The small man's eyes flickered as the fly droned past his face. Sanjeev held his breath as the fly began to drop down towards the small man's scythe. Lower it dropped, lower still, but instead of settling, it glided on. Past one scythe, past another, and another. Then it landed.

'Don't move!' hissed the captain. 'Stay completely still.'

Everyone watched the blow fly as it crawled slowly across the scythe of the tallest farmer. A moment later, another blow fly landed on the same scythe, then another and another till there was a mass of buzzing green on that scythe and that one alone. The tallest farmer stared hard at the captain. The farmer's mouth opened and closed, but no words came out. The captain stepped forward, but faster than anyone could react, the farmer launched himself at the nearest soldier on horseback. Reaching up and grabbing the soldier by the neck, the farmer hauled him off his horse. In the blink of an eye, he'd jumped into the saddle. Kicking back two soldiers with his feet, the farmer dug his heels into the horse and galloped away.

'You, you and you. After him!' ordered the captain, pointing at three soldiers who immediately galloped after the farmer. The captain turned to Sanjeev. 'We'll catch him, you can be sure of that.'

Sanjeev felt his shoulders relax and his heart beat slow considerably as the metaphorical rope around his neck slipped away. Those hours on the internet researching Song Ci had paid off.

'Sir, if I may…?' Brother Thomas, who had stepped out of the line, put his big head between the captain and Sanjeev.

'What is it?' snapped the captain.

'If our servant has been any trouble to you,' Brother Thomas said, giving Sanjeev a vicious sneer, 'I will only be too glad to beat him…'

'Trouble, did you say?'

Brother Thomas's face went slack. He had made a mistake and he knew it. 'Of course, if he has pleased you,' Brother Thomas said quickly, 'I shall reward him. We must carry both the stick and the carrot, must we not? A servant must know his good deeds will be rewarded and his bad deeds will…'

'Shut up,' said the captain.

Brother Thomas shut up.

'If I had a servant as clever as yours, I would consider myself a lucky man. Do you have any idea how the murderer was caught?'

Brother Thomas opened his mouth, thought for a second, and closed it again. He shook his head.

'Did you know flies can smell blood from far away?'

'No, sir. I didn't know that.'

'Well, it's true. If you have ever been on a battlefield, you will know how quickly the flies come. Even the smallest amount of blood will attract them. Your servant reminded me of these facts. That is how we identified the murderer.'

Brother Thomas was nodding as though he understood everything. 'I see, I see… But why did the fly land on the scythe?'

Behind the brothers, the captain shook his head and walked away. 'You men, wait here. I haven't finished with you yet,' he said, addressing the farmers. As he spoke, his lieutenant approached him and handed over a large, squarish bag.

Brother Thomas was still staring at Sanjeev, totally confused. Brothers Luke and Mark were standing next to him, also looking puzzled. None of them had seen what was happening behind them.

Sanjeev sighed and continued. 'The scythe was the murder weapon. The farmer had cleaned it, but there was still a tiny amount of blood on it – enough for the flies to smell it. All the farmers swore they had their own scythe, remember? Whichever scythe attracted the flies was the one the murderer used to kill the messenger.'

Over Brother Thomas's shoulder, he could see the captain taking something out of the bag and examining it. Was it the messenger's bag? There hadn't been time to see it properly but Sanjeev was sure he'd seen one when the messenger had ridden past. He'd been carrying it, strapped to his back. A squarish, brown bag...

CHAPTER 29

━

As the two soldiers continued to talk in low voices, Brother Mark and Brother Luke turned, following Sanjeev's eyes.

'Oh!' cried Brother Mark when he saw the bag and almost dropping his crutch, he leaned on Brother Luke who looked equally shaky on his feet.

Brother Thomas's head snapped around. His jaw immediately dropped, and he made a sound like a sick kitten.

Frozen to the spot, the three of them watched through staring eyes as the captain nodded, issued a command to the lieutenant, and strode back towards Sanjeev. The three brothers were cowering as though a grizzly bear was approaching. *What was going on?* Somehow the captain didn't seem to notice or care how weirdly the brothers were acting.

'It's the messenger's bag,' the captain said, addressing Sanjeev. 'It's empty apart from some pieces of bloodied scroll. One of the scraps is part of an order to detain someone, and it bears the seal of an official – a judge perhaps. Sadly, there is no information about who is being sought. I've asked my lieutenant to look for the other scrolls but' – he waved a hand – 'the light is disappearing fast.'

At hearing this news, the brothers seemed to relax and began smiling knowingly at each other.

The captain threw Brother Thomas a warning look and turned to Sanjeev. 'Who took the scrolls? Do you have any idea?'

Sanjeev nodded. 'I think it was the murderer.'

The captain looked at Sanjeev disbelievingly. 'Why would he do that? What use would a poor, illiterate farmer have for scrolls? And how do you know it was him?'

'There are traces of blood on the remaining pieces of scroll, right?'

The captain nodded.

'Which suggests the blood came from the murderer's hands.'

The captain gave Sanjeev a calculating look. 'I suppose that makes sense...' he said. 'But I have to ask the same question again: why would a poor farmer who can't read take the scrolls?'

Sanjeev, remembering the words Sherlock Holmes used in these situations, said, 'Once you eliminate the impossible, whatever remains, no matter how improbable, must be the truth. I know it seems unlikely, but there can only be one reason why the farmer took them: he can—'

'Read!' cried the captain.

'Perhaps there was some valuable information in those scrolls?' continued Sanjeev.

'Of course! Of course!' The captain nodded in agreement. 'Why else? But where are they? Where are the... Oh!' he exclaimed. 'Oh no! How stupid!' He slammed his fist into his hand.

Sanjeev nodded. 'There's only one place they can be – on him. He must have hidden it under his clothes.'

The captain's jaw tightened and his eyes glared in the direction of the farmer's escape. He turned back to Sanjeev. He smiled and gave Sanjeev an appreciative look. 'For a slave, you are remarkably sagacious.'

Sanjeev wasn't exactly sure what sagacious meant, but he knew what he *hoped* it meant. 'Um... thanks.'

'The question is,' the captain mused, 'what valuable piece of information might the murderer have discovered on the scrolls? It must have involved some sort of reward perhaps?'

Sanjeev and the captain stood gazing at one another while their brains churned, trying to figure out what the murderer had found. Finally, the captain gave up. 'Enough! It is almost night.' He turned to the remaining farmers. 'You must take me to your village. I must speak with your head man about what has happened here today. There's a chance this murderer may go there. As for you,' addressing Sanjeev once again, 'you and your companions are free to go.'

'Thank you very much, Captain!' cried Brother Thomas.

Sanjeev too thanked the captain, as did the other brothers, who were grovelling and eagerly praising the captain for having 'such great kindness' and 'such immense wisdom'.

Paying no attention to the brothers, the captain gave Sanjeev a sharp salute, turned on his heels, and marched away.

'Let's get out of here before he changes his mind,' Brother Mark said in a low voice and pointed his crutch. 'We'll continue along the valley and camp near the river once it is fully dark.' The other brothers grunted their agreement.

As Sanjeev walked towards Daisy, he wondered yet again when, or if, this crazy adventure would end. Behind him, he could hear the captain giving more orders. A moment later, the dull thunder of horses' hooves filled the edge of the forest; when Sanjeev turned, the soldiers had already galloped out of the forest and into the valley, their captain at the front. Minutes later, the dusk had swallowed them.

CHAPTER 30

Sanjeev squeezed his knees against Daisy's bony back. With a grunt, she straightened her hind legs, which pitched Sanjeev towards her ears. Then she straightened her front legs, which rocked Sanjeev backwards. But Sanjeev was used to all of it now. Daisy turned and fluttered her eyelids. Sanjeev reached out and patted her muscular neck.

Brother Thomas turned and gave Sanjeev a sour look. 'Hurry up! Let's go,' Brother Mark shouted from the front, and slowly the little caravan of four moved forward. This time, Daisy and Sanjeev were last. As usual, Sanjeev perched on a woven blanket with all sorts of bags tied across it. As Daisy followed the swishing tail of the camel in front of her, Sanjeev wobbled back and forth, side to side. Soon they had passed beneath the canopy of the last tree and had put the forest behind them.

While Daisy followed the rest, Sanjeev's mind wandered to the monkey key again. He could still sense the weight of it in his hands and, inexplicably, he felt a deep melancholy at having let it slip from his hands. But he shook himself out of these crazy thoughts. The key wasn't his! Why on earth was he getting so attached to a piece of metal he'd only seen for a minute or so? And he was probably hallucinating about the movement in the key. He was sure his blood sugar must be pretty low. His last meal seemed hours and hours ago.

Sanjeev grew irritated. He wanted to stop. He wanted to eat. He wanted to get off Daisy and stretch his limbs. Not only that, it was so dark he could barely make out the hunched, swaying figures of the three brothers and their camels in front of him. And poor Daisy – she must have been as exhausted as he was. He'd felt a real kinship with her over the days they had been together, as if she understood him in a way the others didn't. Just like the understanding he'd had with Jigsaw – a shared feeling that went beyond words. She responded to his pat by raising her head and loudly blowing air out of her nostrils.

Thinking of Jigsaw brought back a torrent of feelings and images. It was as if a door had opened in his mind and he had stepped through. He remembered how upset he'd been when he discovered Jigsaw was missing, which made him feel guilty for not thinking more about him. Then, as if it were a dream inside a dream, another image came to him – the mosaic of the woman in white that hung in the gallery. Her dress had a sheen to it that made it glow, almost like a beacon. It had pulled at him, tugging him forwards.

Daisy lurched, kicking up dust. It was crazy travelling on these rough tracks without lights. Why were the brothers insisting on it? He coughed as the dust caught in his throat and wished there was a car window he could close. The moon was rising, bright and full, but even so, a couple of halogen headlights would come in handy right about now. He gave a weary chuckle. There were quite a few things other things he would like to invent: cushions for camel saddles, and a saddlebag candy dispenser, and a camel suspension system to stop the seat swinging about. He sighed. If he was going to be trapped in this space-time bubble, he'd better come up with better ideas than those!

A different thought crossed his mind. He had never thought about it before, but did flies have noses? He was sure they didn't have ones exactly like humans, but what did they have? Did they smell with their antenna? Probably, but he would have to check it out on Wikipedia…

He stopped. He knew where his mind was going: back to New Jersey. *No!* he told himself. *I have to focus on where I am – right here, right now. I have to concentrate on surviving.*

Sanjeev looked up. A bolt of panic shot through him. The brothers were no longer in sight. He couldn't hear them anymore either. He'd been so preoccupied with his thoughts he hadn't taken any notice of where he and Daisy were going. He looked left and right. The narrow path they were on was bound on either side by walls of rock, full of deep crags and sharp, jutting edges. It seemed like he and Daisy had veered away from the valley floor and the river, and wandered deeper into the foothills. But how long had they been following a different path? How far ahead were the others? He had lost all sense of time.

He heard a sudden clanking that echoed along the rock walls. Startled, Daisy drew back quickly, stepping on a rock that shifted beneath her front left hoof. Sanjeev, frightened by the sound as well, mistakenly tilted towards the left, throwing Daisy further off balance. She hit the side of the rocky wall with a heavy thud, the flank of her leg banging against an outcropping rock.

Daisy gave a soft moan and staggered away from the stone, jerking wildly as she tried to regain her footing. Sanjeev tried to help her steady herself but realised he could help best by allowing his body to relax and letting her find her centre. When she did, she was limping.

They were lucky – not much farther ahead there was a welcome sight and sound: the tinkling of falling water as it ran, silvery with moonlight, down a wall of stone. In spite of his fear, Sanjeev remembered how thirsty he was.

Directing Daisy towards the water, he whispered the command to kneel. Daisy was eager to comply. At a lopsided tilt, she awkwardly lowered herself down to her knees and drank. Sanjeev dismounted quickly, but instead of going to drink he went to her side. Blood matted the fur on her left flank and had run down her leg, staining her hoof. In the moonlight he could see the wound was open – a dark, messy, gaping cut.

CHAPTER 31

The wave of nausea hit Sanjeev, almost knocking him over. This was more than bad, it was gross; *totally* gross. He bent over, put his hands on his knees and tried to catch his breath. Then he thought about how much pain Daisy must be feeling. Compared to her suffering, his discomfort was nothing! How could he think about himself when she was injured so badly?

Sanjeev heard no noise other than the loud beating of his heart. Whatever was clanging from behind, whatever it was that had spooked him and Daisy, appeared to be gone now. Still too scared to move, he decided to stay quiet and make sure they were safe before helping her.

Taking a deep breath, he straightened up and put his hand against Daisy's side. She was breathing heavily, moving her head from him as if to avoid pain. Sanjeev spoke to her in soft tones as he stroked her neck. She looked at him and saw recognition in her eyes. Her breathing slowed.

What could he do? He had no styptic pen, no medicine of any sort. The most important thing was to clean it. Clean it and cover it so it wouldn't get infected. He had no idea of how long it would take to get to Byzantium, or wherever it was they were headed. But until they could get hold of some herbs, some medicine, this was the best he could do.

He took one of his trouser legs in both hands and ripped it off just below the knee. The fabric, worn from the many miles of travel, gave way easily and he was able to tear its cloth into thick strips. He soaked the cloth in the water. Then he took the ropes of her halter in his left hand and began to wash the area around the wound. When Daisy pulled away, Sanjeev gave a steady tug on the halter, so she knew he wanted her to stay kneeling. He moved closer to the wound, cleaning off her fur, until he was able to wash her wound directly. He felt his stomach turn again. Surprisingly, Daisy had calmed down. Sanjeev thought perhaps it was because she trusted him. He squeezed the bloody water out of the cloth, soaked it with clean water and, with his fingers gently touching, did his best to make sure the wound was free of grit.

Knotting a number of strips of cloth in place, he carefully strung them together to form one longer piece. He needed to tear more fabric from his trousers to make it long enough to circle her thigh a couple of times. Holding a damp rag over the wound with one hand, he used his other hand to loop the long strip around her leg, weaving it over and under so it would stay in place.

He hummed to her as he worked, doing his best to comfort Daisy while he tied the cloth strip. It had to be tight, but not too tight. It seemed snug, but not painfully so. He tested it to see if it would stay. It would have to do.

He stood up, placed his hand upon her neck. 'That better, girl?' he asked gently.

In the silver haze of the moon, Daisy looked at him through her thick lashes, the fear in her eyes gone. He gathered his things, making sure to top off his water bag. His stomach gave a low growl. His nausea had disappeared completely and in its place was a desire to eat anything he could possibly get his hands on. He looked at the saddlebags. A moment later, he was stuffing his face with dried biscuits and gulping down water. Even though he could have eaten every one of the biscuits, he was careful only to eat his share and no more.

When his portion was gone, he commanded Daisy to stand, his voice firm but gentle. She rose slowly, shuffled a bit to gain her balance and looked at him, her dark eyes barely visible in the gloom.

Still dismounted, Sanjeev surveyed the path they were on. The moonlight showed a thread woven through a dizzying set of switchbacks, and caverns that climbed higher into the foothills above them – not the way they wanted to go! Below them, the moon sparkled on the river. They needed to get back onto the valley floor.

Soon, they were moving again, but slowly – half the speed they'd been travelling at before – heading back the way they had come, Sanjeev walking at Daisy's side. Hopefully, they would soon find the point at which their path had diverged from the one the brothers had taken.

He wondered if the brothers had even noticed they were no longer following behind them. Probably not! But even if they cared little for him, he was the one carrying the dried biscuits. That thought made him smirk and he felt more upbeat as he and Daisy continued on the path through the darkness, her leathery pads and feet making regular rustling sounds as they brushed against the hardened soil.

Something – a faint rustle? – made the hairs on the back of his neck stand up. But as he was preparing to turn, fists tight, ready to fight, someone wrapped his hands around Sanjeev's neck and squeezed hard.

Sanjeev struggled, kicking, trying to punch his attacker – incredibly difficult to do with the attacker behind him. He tried frantically to pull his attacker's arms apart, bucked his whole body back to try to dislodge his assailant. The hold around his neck tightened and Sanjeev started feeling faint as his oxygen supply dwindled. His body went limp and his eyes closed. A remote part of his brain registered that he was dying far from home and there was absolutely no one to help him…

CHAPTER 32

—

Sanjeev found himself collapsed on the ground, gasping and gulping in air. In the moonlight, his attacker lay sprawled against the side of the path, his head leaning against the cliff that the track had been cut into. Daisy must have knocked him out with a kick! Sanjeev struggled up, and swaying a little, he stared at the man's face. He took a step back. It was the murderer. One part of Sanjeev's mind hoped the man was dead: he'd murdered the messenger and attacked him only moments ago. But another part was relieved: he didn't want to be responsible for killing someone or dealing with a dead body. The man's hand twitched; he groaned.

Jumping onto Daisy, Sanjeev started down the path at a steady trot, leaving the writhing man behind them. He had to find the brothers and warn them before the murderer came to.

He soon heard them even before he saw them. He had been steadily descending to the valley floor, carefully but quickly leading Daisy down the hillside, and had passed a huge boulder when he heard Brother Thomas's voice, mumbling angrily, '—will wish he was dead if he isn't already!'

They plodded around the massive stone, and there were the dark figures of the three brothers. They had laid out their bedding and tethered their camels in the clearing. For once, Sanjeev was relieved to see them.

'Where have you been?' Brother Thomas roared, sitting up and pointing. 'We've been looking for you! We need to eat and sleep now for an early start!'

'The murderer attacked me. The camel knocked him out,' Sanjeev spluttered, standing close to Daisy, feeling her warmth against his side. He was shaking and babbling now, the fear still in him from his near-death experience, 'I didn't know what to do. She was hurt, and we stopped so I could clean her wound, but I'm sure the murderer will wake up soon. Please do something! He tried to strangle me! I tried to fight back, but he'll be awake again soon. He'll come here and kill us all!'

Brother Thomas leaned down to look at the blood-stained bandages tied around Daisy's leg. 'Where did you leave him?' he asked quietly. Sanjeev pointed into the darkness towards the path he and Daisy had come down. The brothers looked at each other and nodded.

'Boy, we can tell you are quite shaken up. Stay here and rest, and we'll go and handle the murderer. It's the same man from the village? Are you sure? The one who has the scrolls? You're absolutely sure?' Brother Mark asked.

'Yes, yes, the same man. I'm very, very certain.' Sanjeev nodded repeatedly; grateful the brothers were going to deal with his attacker. How drained he felt. All he wanted to do was check on Daisy's wound and wake up from this nightmare.

The brothers mounted, turned their camels around and trekked back the way Sanjeev and Daisy had come. He was upset to see them all go and wished one of them had stayed behind – even Brother Thomas would have been fine. At least when he was with them, he felt a bit safer. Being alone with Daisy in the dark countryside was spooky as the silence closed around them.

Ages later, the brothers still hadn't returned. *Certainly taking their time* thought Sanjeev. He wondered if he should go and see whether he could find them. But what if he got lost? What if the brothers returned by a different route? What if they had decided to make camp and he and Daisy stumbled past them without realising it? No, it was better to sit tight and wait. He rubbed his neck. It hurt. The last thing he wanted to do was get back on Daisy and make her walk with her injury. And anyway, he was too exhausted to move. He should be patient. They were bound to come back sooner or later…

'Boy!' a voice barked.

Sanjeev awoke with a start. He must have dozed off, resting against Daisy's warm body as she lay on the ground. He gave a soft moan in reply.

The voice continued, 'Enough of your laziness! Get up! We need to collect wood for the fire!'

Sanjeev was shaken roughly. He opened his eyes. The face in front of him said, 'Wood. Now!'

'What happened to the murderer? Did you find him? Where is he? Will he attack us again?' Sanjeev jolted wide awake.

'We don't need to worry about him anymore. No more questions! Get the wood now!'

Sanjeev felt his stomach heave as he got to his feet and stumbled out of the camp into the darkness. The moon, barely visible, hung above his head like the curved blade of a knife. He walked a short distance, realising too late he should have brought a lit branch to use as a torch. Something told him not to return to Brother Thomas empty-handed.

He walked a bit farther slowly, the land before him watched over by a star-filled sky. He mumbled. Disconnected thoughts flitted through his mind. Dark clouds partly covered the light cast by the moon, which was barely enough to see a mountain, let alone enough to spot pieces of firewood.

He walked a bit further, tripped again, and landed on his knees. This time the clatter sounded different. He reached down and groped around until he found a few pieces of scattered wood. *This will have to do,* he thought, gathering them up. He turned back, trying not to drop any. He picked out the feeble light of the fire in the gloom and quickly made his way toward it. As he walked, he saw three men hard at work at the very edge of the ring of light cast by the campfire.

He walked closer, puzzled, wondering… Sanjeev crept a little closer and stopped. 'Oh!' he gasped. The three brothers were kneeling, scrabbling at loose soil, digging with their hands, pushing away earth while a lifeless form lay next to them. They looked up in unison at Sanjeev. Brother Thomas beckoned him with his hands. "Well, since you're back too soon, come, Boy! We have some more work for you!'

Walking with wooden legs, very slowly, Sanjeev approached the three brothers, barely breathing watching them continue their gruesome task. 'Get in the hole and dig, it needs to be deeper Boy,' Brother Thomas said threateningly. The three brothers sat on the edge of the hole, back lit by the fire, still breathing hard from the effort of digging. They watched intently as Sanjeev scrabbled at the soil with his bare hands, occasionally cutting his fingers on a small sharp stone as he dug, throwing handfuls of soil onto the growing pile. His arms and shoulders ached but he was numb, an automaton.

'Alright, that's enough!' Sanjeev hauled himself up the side. 'You and Brother Luke hold the arms and Brother Mark and I will do the legs.' The body was heavy and already stiff as a board. Sanjeev got hold of the left arm. It was cold and smooth. Soundlessly, they swung the body up and over the hole, and let go. Sanjeev heard a soft thud. That done, Brother Mark started picking up several objects scattered on the ground. And yet again, Brother Mark walking without his crutch…

'We'll burn the scrolls,' Brother Thomas said impatiently. 'Fill it up Boy!' Brother Thomas walked over to the fire and threw the scrolls on the flames, which flared briefly.

Sanjeev, Mark and Luke worked in silence as they piled soil on top of the body. Once the body was well and truly buried, Brother Mark looked over at Sanjeev coldly, 'We still have a long way to go, Boy. Don't speak of this to anyone or try and run away. It would be unfortunate for anything else to happen to you.'

Sanjeev cried himself to sleep that night, quiet deep sobs racked his thin frame. Burying a murdered body had broken something in him, he was longer a child. Forces he didn't understand were dragging him down a path he had never foreseen in his fourteen years, and his usual cheery demeanour and problem-solving attitude was no match for the horrors he had seen this day.

Chapter 33

The next day Daisy was having some trouble walking normally because she was favouring her uninjured leg, which made sitting on her even trickier than usual. Sanjeev was having to hold on so tight he wondered if his legs would ever straighten out again. He was still in deep shock from everything he had witnessed the day before.

As the day wore on, Sanjeev's head began to pound. He didn't want to upset the brothers. He was subdued, knowing he was in the company of killers. But, at last, he spoke up. 'I need to rest. So does my camel.'

Brother Mark did not want to stop. 'No, let's keep going. A few more days hard riding and we'll be there.' Wild with excitement, he shouted at the others. 'Can't you smell the reward?'

Sanjeev's ears perked up. *Reward? What reward?*

'We can stop for a little while only,' Brother Thomas said coldly, and few minutes later, all of them had dismounted and were standing beside their camels.

'You mentioned a reward… What reward?' Sanjeev asked as they tethered the camels.

Brother Luke, who was standing next to Sanjeev, gave him a panicked look. He opened his mouth, but Brother Mark cut in. 'It's none of your concern, Boy! Stop asking questions!' His forehead, Sanjeev noticed, was stained by a fresh dark bruise, purple and red. Sanjeev had a sudden urge to punch him hard and keep punching till all of Brother Thomas's face was bruised the same purple. He wanted to shout and scream at him and tell him he wasn't real. Brother Thomas only existed in Sanjeev's brain. He hadn't really helped to bury a murdered person for reasons no one would tell him. This was a nightmare and he would wake up soon, back in New Jersey.

But all Sanjeev did was clench his fists and tighten his jaw. Whatever this was, he needed to survive it.

Brother Thomas growled at Sanjeev. 'I'll rattle whatever brains you have if you say another word.'

Sanjeev, quickly putting his head down, removed Daisy's bandages and used some water to clean the cut out again. The wound was still bloody but didn't look infected. 'We still have a long way to go,' he whispered to Daisy, patting her neck. 'I sure hope nothing else happens to you, or me.'

Days went past. Then weeks. Daisy grew stronger. The four of them journeyed out of one valley and into others even longer, even greener. The rivers gathered more tributaries, widened and meandered.

They too were seeking the sea…

Brother Thomas rose off his saddle and pointed, his voice shrill with excitement. 'I see it! I can see Galata and the city walls beyond!'

They were on top of a small hill, farmland spreading out before them. Was it Sanjeev's imagination, or could he really smell the sea? Images of crashing waves and swirling tides filled his head.

'Soon it'll be time for you to take a rest, eh, girl?' Sanjeev said wearily.

Galata – a settlement on the eastern shore of the Bosphorus Straits – was all the three brothers had chattered about for days. According to them, a short journey across the straits to its western shore and they would be in Byzantium, or Constantinople as it was now called, the greatest city on Earth. As Sanjeev gazed at the glimmering horizon where the distant pale blue of the sea dissolved into the sky, he imagined what life must be like inside Byzantium. A fact, from where he couldn't remember, popped into his head. Chariot races! The ancient Romans loved them and so did the people of Byzantium. Would there be a chariot race when he got there? Maybe there was one happening right now at the Hippodrome. Just imagine 150,000 people cheering, half the population of the city, as teams of horses raced like crazy around the stadium.

'Hey!'

Sanjeev's imagined crowds disappeared. Turning, he stared at Brother Thomas whose face was contorted into a shape Sanjeev hadn't seen before – joy.

'Get that camel of yours moving faster!' Brother Thomas said. 'I want to be there *now.*' And with that, he lashed at his camel, prompting it into a fast trot. The two others did the same and raced ahead. Brother Thomas's camel was completely healthy; Brother Luke's and Brother Marks too. But what about his? What about Daisy? Sanjeev sighed. How could people be so inconsiderate towards animals?

'Get a move on!' Brother Thomas cried, turning in his saddle and calling back to Sanjeev. 'Or I'm going make you walk and have that camel for dinner.'

'Sorry, Daisy,' Sanjeev said. And he truly was. Reluctantly, he dug his heels into her and urged her forward, following the three brothers as they practically galloped towards the strait.

It was several hours later when they finally arrived at the shores of the Bosphorus. The road that took them up alongside the strait was choked with boats. Most were simple single-sail craft, their bows and sterns curling up and making them look a little like floating bananas. But not all were small. One of the biggest was long and sleek with around fifty oars: each plunging, pulling, and rising in unison. Its bow sliced like a blade through the blue and even the brothers stopped and watched as it glided past, its tall prow pointing towards the broader channel and its deep, rough water.

As they continued towards the crossing point, Sanjeev gazed across the body of water sloshing lazily against the rocks next to the towering walls that rose on the shore opposite. He couldn't imagine how any army could break through them and get inside the city.

'Up there!' Brother Luke pointed. Ahead, a boat, smaller than the long elegant one that had passed but still with over ten oars, was pulling into a dock.

'Our ferry,' said Brother Luke.

'Now all we need to do is arrange a good price,' said Brother Thomas. The way he said it, Sanjeev imagined they would haggle the whole afternoon. Fortunately, it did not take long to arrange passage, and all the way across the strait, Sanjeev stayed beside Daisy, comforting her as the boat rocked and dipped and its oars plunged and rose. Despite the natural beauty of the water, two questions nagged at Sanjeev: would the brothers release him? Would they sell him to someone else, as Brother Thomas had threatened to do? No point in asking them. They'd only tell him to shut up or hit him. The brothers, lying flat on their backs on the boat's wooden deck, had all closed their eyes.

The sun, reflecting off the water, pressed deep into Sanjeev's eyes. Lying down next to Daisy, he closed his eyes too and let the rhythm of the water soothe him.

When they finally landed on the other shore, they watered the camels in a fast-flowing stream, mounted and continued on their way. Sanjeev felt wearier than any other time he could remember. But soon enough they were there: the city of Constantinople.

'The Walls of Theodosius and the Charisius Gate!' Brother Thomas yelled, pointing to the city's first and greatest line of defence either side of them as they passed through the checkpoint and into the city.

Sanjeev clapped Daisy on the neck. Even she seemed amazed by what she was seeing as she clomped past the guards and along the narrow, thronging street. Had everyone suddenly decided to come out of their houses and into the streets or was it always this busy? There were shops and dogs and houses and the air smelled of fresh bread and fruit and horses and… he wrinkled his nose… other nauseating stuff too.

The city reminded Sanjeev of paintings and movies he'd seen about Rome, but… different. The buildings looked similar, and the togas, and the woven hairstyles that looked like judges' wigs. But there was something else. He remembered what he'd heard at school about the city being at the crossroads of the East and West. That's what it was – Constantinople, was the way it was because it wasn't Rome. It was how Romans had adapted to the life and culture of the East.

As they walked through the bustle and noise, no one paid them any attention. There were other camels around, other religious figures, other people as dusty and travel-worn. Indeed, if their clothing was any guide, there seemed to be as many foreign travellers as citizens.

They led their camels down more narrow, cobbled streets until they were in sight of the palace. The splendour of the building and finely manicured gardens took Sanjeev's breath away. He drew Daisy to a halt to take it all in. As he sat, a horn call went up. And then another.

Within moments the brothers and Sanjeev were surrounded by guards with golden breastplates and helmets that shone in the sun.

'Dismount your camels and leave them with my men here. You are to be escorted to Emperor Justinian.'

Sanjeev wasn't happy about leaving Daisy, but he had no choice. He gave her two big pats on the neck and told her he'd be back soon.

Her eyes remained on him as the soldiers led her away.

CHAPTER 34

—

The palace, a great space lit by rows of thin windows that pierced the walls, dwarfed all the buildings around it. Sanjeev marvelled at the width of the columns that held the roof aloft. He followed them up to high ceilings painted with pictures of royalty – men wearing wreaths on their brows, their bodies draped in flowing togas. Images adorned the floor as well. It was a giant mosaic, made of countless tiles pieced together in ornate, floral patterns that echoed the images on the walls – gryphons, peacocks and hawks grasping snakes in their talons.

They followed the guards, crossing under arches made of alternating brown and white stone. Word of their arrival had preceded them. Above the arches, on the second storey, were more arches, filled with people jostling to get a look at the newcomers. Many of them were pointing at the monks, at him, all talking so loudly Sanjeev couldn't make out more than a few words here and there.

'Back at last!'

'—didn't think we'd ever see—'

'—might not make it.'

Sanjeev looked at the lords and ladies, then down at his clothes. The journey had not treated them well. Not only was the fabric fraying apart from where he'd torn off Daisy's bandage, but there were places – on his elbows and knees – where the fabric had just about worn through. Worse yet – he stunk, almost as much as if he'd been travelling on the back of a camel and hadn't taken a shower for weeks. And compared to the people around him in their light, shimmering silk robes, their sandalwood perfumes and unguents and hair glistening with olive oil, he smelled even worse. He'd got used to the smell out on the trail, even come to love Daisy's musky odour. Now he wanted to take a *very* long shower.

The hall opened out onto a great room ringed by balconies, filled with chattering people. Sanjeev and the brothers stopped before a wide clearing, empty but for a raised platform in the centre. Upon this dais, a man was lying on his side on a gold jewel-encrusted divan couch. He was enveloped in a robe of deep purple embroidered with more jewels. Around his neck, a giant stone hung at the end of a gold cord. Despite all the noise filling the hall around him, his eyes were closed.

Beside him stood another man, gently plucking the strings of a lyre as he sang. The man on the divan waited for the song to finish before he opened his eyes. Flanking him on either side of the platform, stood a pair of guards, their spears in hand. Next to one of them was a woman dressed in a robe so white it seemed to glow.

'Thank you, Fabius,' he said. 'Truly, Heaven will welcome you – you already sing with the voice of an angel.'

With a deep bow, Fabius stepped off the dais and joined the others at the sides of the court.

A man stepped forward into the empty space before the dais, took a knee and bowed his head. A hush filled the palace hall.

'I wish to speak with Emperor Justinian with some important news,' he said.

The emperor, irritated from being pulled from his reverie, did not move other than to swivel his head slightly. He looked down his nose at the man before him.

'Yes, Septimus?' he said.

Septimus, head still bowed, spoke loudly, his voice echoing off the mosaic floor. 'The envoys have returned at last, your holiness!'

At this, Emperor Justinian sat up quickly and leaned forward.

The rough hands that had grabbed the monks and Sanjeev shoved them forward, out past the perimeter of the crowd and into the space before the emperor.

A tall woman stepped forward beside the emperor.

'Hail, intrepid travellers!' Justinian said. 'Although we are eager to hear your tales of adventure, they will have to wait.' His eyes were bright with excitement. 'Do you have it? You do, yes? It's all been worth it... Has it not?' The tone of the man's question was a little threatening.

The tall woman beside him replied quickly. 'My emperor, we promised you two years ago we would bring you what you desired. My agents have fulfilled that promise.'

Sanjeev leaned forward. Looking along the line, he saw the woman's face in profile.

'Good,' said the emperor. 'I am glad to hear it, my Lady Antonina.' Sanjeev refocused on him. 'Well, let's see them!'

'Of course, my emperor,' replied Lady Antonina. She snapped her fingers, and Brother Mark stepped forward. Sanjeev looked at Lady Antonina again.

The woman's face, her dress... Like a train hurtling into Grand Central station, Sanjeev suddenly remembered where he had seen her before: it was the woman in the mosaic at the Met museum!

CHAPTER 35

—

He couldn't believe he was looking right at the woman in the brown and white dress from the mosaic! He gazed around: soldiers standing with swords dangling at their sides; people talking in excited whispers; women wearing long dresses and brightly-coloured hats; a throne; a man with a crown and grey, rat-tail hair; the people wearing robes tied at the waist.

He stared at Lady Antonina, then Brother Mark. The monk was grinning and slowly twisting off the top of his crutch – the part that fitted below his armpit. Sanjeev realised, as Brother Mark began dismantling it, that it was hollow. Brother Mark was frowning, poking around inside, and frowning... Then he was smiling! Smiling and pulling things out. Whatever they were, he had them cupped in his hands. They looked like rags. The rest of the crutch clattered onto the stone floor. Everyone ignored it; everyone, including Sanjeev, was focused on the rags.

Carefully, Brother Mark took one and began folding it back. At the centre of the rag was a small box. Sanjeev realised that he, and just about everyone else in the room, was hardly breathing. Gently, Brother Mark opened the box and tipped some small whitish-grey objects onto Lady Antonina's hand. Lady Antonina smiled and, like in the dream, she held the contents of the box in the air. Suddenly, everyone cheered. Even the emperor was bouncing up and down on his seat.

'What's this all about?' Sanjeev yelled to Brother Thomas. 'What's that?'

Brother Thomas looked at Sanjeev as though he were the dumbest creature in creation. 'It's silk, of course!'

'Silk?' repeated Sanjeev. 'What do you mean, silk?'

For a moment, Brother Thomas's grizzled face stared back at him and when Sanjeev thought he would not answer, he did something totally unexpected: he smiled. Sanjeev was taken aback. Obviously, Brother Thomas was feeling very, very pleased with himself. 'Those are silkworm eggs, stupid: the first to have been smuggled out of China. Hiding the eggs inside a crutch and dressing as monks. Ha! What brilliance – even if I say so myself. Thanks to us, Byzantium can make its own silk. And in a moment, the Emperor Justinian will reward the Lady Antonina, and the Lady Antonina will reward us. We'll be rich and you...' he said, his grin souring, 'you will be sold.'

'What?' Sanjeev cried. 'You can't do that!'

Brother Thomas gave a chortle and along with Brother Mark and Brother Luke, joined Lady Antonina, who had approached the throne to give the emperor a better view of the silkworm eggs that she still held in her hands. The lords and ladies, desperate to get a better look at what the agents of Lady Antonina had brought back from China, were chattering like sparrows.

The emperor looked down at the dozen black silkworm eggs that filled Lady Antonina's hands. 'What is this?' he said with disbelief. 'You were to discover how the silk was made and... you bring me this?' His face clouded with anger. 'Dare you mock me?'

Brother Mark bowed his head. 'No, your holiness. These eggs will hatch into silkworms that are the source of silk.'

The emperor remained unconvinced. 'But how?'

'The worms wrap themselves in it, emperor, when it is time for them to become moths. China has perfected a system for unwinding it and weaving it into cloth.'

The emperor raised his eyebrows. 'Silk… from worms? However, did they come by this knowledge?'

Unlike his fellow travellers, Brother Mark had made an effort to learn as much as possible during their time in the East. 'It is said that Lei Zu, the wife of the Yellow Emperor, plucked a cocoon from her boiling tea as it unravelled. From this she learned that the cocoon was made of a single thread.'

'A single thread? Surely our clothes are not made of one strand of fibre,' said Lady Antonina.

'No, my lady, several fibres are wound together to make the thread.'

It was Lady Antonina's turn to be surprised. 'It is difficult to imagine.'

'Just as we wrap ourselves in togas, the worm dresses itself in a cocoon of cloth,' Brother Mark said, head cast down.

'Hm,' the emperor said. He took another look at the eggs and leaned back on his divan. 'Excellent. Your services will be well rewarded.' He gestured for the captain of the guards to come to him. 'See that these men are paid a hundred times the weight of the box of cocoons in gold.'

He turned to Lady Antonina. 'You will oversee the silk making.'

Brother Mark took a step forward, an action that did not go unnoticed by the guards. They gripped their spears tightly, ready to defend their emperor.

'Emperor…' Brother Mark began. 'Perhaps I haven't made myself clear,' he added hastily. 'I can assure you it is not as easy as it seems.'

Emperor Justinian was not convinced. 'We hatch them, we grow the worms, we remove their silk and grow more. Isn't that all?'

'Yes, emperor, but if we hope to harvest the silk, we must treat the worms properly.'

'Treat the worms properly?'

'Indeed, proper care for the worms extends as far as seeing to the air that flows past them, the smells they breathe. Even the noises they are exposed to affect the worms' appetite.'

'Who would have thought they were such sensitive creatures?' Lady Antonina said. 'These are the secrets the silk people have kept guarded so long?'

'Yes, my lady. The process requires great precision. Achieving the highest quality silk will not be a simple task. Even the trees must be tended properly. The Seres have a god of the silkworm, my lady, named Jung-Jui, who presides over the mulberry groves. These they consider sacred.'

Lady Antonina looked again at the treasure she held in her hands. 'The empire has seen great mountains of silver and gold travel east to pay for silk. At last! This tiny mountain of eggs worms will be what we build upon.'

'They will be worth thousands of times their weight in gold – if properly taken care of.' Brother Mark took another step forward and bowed. 'I would be happy to act as adviser in these regards. Surely you would not want to entrust the precious cocoons to anyone who knows any less. The risk is too great.'

Lady Antonina smiled in amusement. 'And why do we need *your* services?'

'Ah, but there are so many ways that our service…' He turned and, upon seeing Brother Thomas, faced Lady Antonina again, placed his hand upon his chest and continued, '*my* service is of the utmost importance. I will tend to the proper handling of the moths and the preparation of the cocoons, ensuring that their numbers increase.'

Brother Luke raised his voice so it carried over to Lady Antonina. 'You will also want someone to oversee the creation and upkeep of the looms I saw in Hangzhou.' He stepped forward past Brother Thomas to stand alongside Brother Mark. 'Either of us would be proud to offer our knowledge and skills.'

Brother Thomas cried out in indignation. 'My lady, this… these scoundrels would have you believe that I am…'

Lady Antonina rolled her eyes and, with a wave of her hand, gestured to the guards. They approached Brother Thomas, who was now cowering in fear, and roughly grabbed each of his arms.

'Of little worth?' she asked.

Brother Thomas crumpled.

Brother Luke, not bothering to hide the look of contempt on his face, watched Brother Thomas. 'I have long known you to be a fool, Thomas. I am glad to be free of you. As for skills, you have none, other than being able to bellow like an injured bull. We were lucky the murderer took the scrolls before the soldiers came, otherwise we would all be swinging from the end of a rope: those scrolls were our arrest warrants. As for how we managed to escape being charged with the murder of the messenger, the *last* person we have you to thank is you!'

'What is this?' the emperor cried, alert again. 'What murderer?'

Brother Luke turned to the emperor and bowed his head before answering. 'Only one of the many difficulties we faced, emperor. A messenger from China ordered our arrest for the theft of the silkworm eggs. A farmer murdered that messenger. The boy proved himself to be most resourceful, helping us to avoid being wrongfully hanged for the killing.'

Sanjeev shrugged, modestly.

'And the actual murderer? What happened to him?' the emperor asked.

'He returned and tried to blackmail us – threatened to tell the army where we were and show them our arrest warrants if we didn't give him money. So, we…' Brother Luke drew an imaginary knife across his throat.

Lady Antonina made a disgusted face and looked directly at Sanjeev, deeply into his eyes as if seeing him for the first time. 'Perhaps we can find some use for this boy. If I understand correctly, the mission would not have been successful were it not for his help.'

'Yes, my lady,' Brother Luke replied.

It took a second for Sanjeev to realise what she meant. Never mind that it sounded positive – there was *no way* he was going to carry on being someone's servant, even if that person was Lady Antonina. He'd spent weeks travelling with the brothers, hoping when they got to Constantinople, they'd set him free or he would wake up.

For a moment the nobles regarded him, some smiling, most frowning. Then their faces lost interest and, jewels sparkling, they turned and began shuffling forward, gathering in an ever-tightening circle around the brothers and Lady Antonina.

Sanjeev swallowed. It was now or never.

CHAPTER 36

━

Slowly, very slowly and without turning around, Sanjeev stepped back from the stage, his leather sandals dragging against the rough stone floor. He glanced over his shoulder. He was getting closer to the throne room's exit – iron-reinforced wooden doors guarded by fierce-looking soldiers. Like excited children, the soldiers were busy trying to see the silkworms and were at least three metres from the doors. Beyond the doors, Sanjeev could see a long corridor with no one in it. Where the corridor went, he had no idea, but it didn't matter as long as it was a way out of the palace. If he could get into the streets, he would disappear. All he needed to do was get out of the throne room. Just a few metres further. A step or two more. He hardly dared to breathe. He glanced again at the door…

'Boy!'

Sanjeev's head snapped around. His rage getting the better of him, Brother Thomas had broken the guards' grip on his arms and was pointing his finger straight at Sanjeev. 'STOP RIGHT THERE!'

The cry bounced around the four stone walls like a rubber ball. The emperor turned. The lords and ladies turned. The guards turned, and seeing what Sanjeev was up to, instantly rushed forward, arms outstretched, snarling like furious bears.

But Sanjeev was already on his toes. Launching himself forward, he dodged one, then the other. The lumbering guards made a grab at him. He ducked, swerved and twisted away, avoiding their outstretched hands and diving into the corridor. Ha! That was almost fun! He stole a backwards glance. The guards were a heap of arms and legs on the floor. He skidded left at the bottom of the corridor and belted down another one. A woman carrying a tray of food came out of a room and shrank back as Sanjeev zoomed past. Panting, he ran towards the end of that corridor. Another intersection. Left again. This time, the corridor had tiny windows along it. Through the windows, he could see a courtyard, a cloister and stone arches, daylight and the palace gardens! But how to get out there?

He continued running. Another intersection, and he turned right, skidding around the corner and almost falling. Behind him, feet were thumping, getting closer. Angry shouts echoed. More corridors. This place was a rabbit warren! He stopped. Which way? Straight on? To the left? To the right? Which way was out?

He stood, gasping for air and listening. He could hear the men chasing him getting closer, their shouts and cries rising louder and louder. He stared down the dimly lit corridor to his left. Voices were coming from one of the rooms.

As though hypnotised, Sanjeev walked along the corridor. With each step, the voices got louder. He stopped and turned. It was coming from the door in front of him. He stared at the door's dark wooden face. Behind it, someone was asking a question. He knew that voice, but whose was it? He had to find out. Sanjeev took hold of the door's handle. He had no choice now. He was trapped. This adventure – dream? Nightmare? – had brought him from central Asia to Byzantium with three silkworm smugglers. And now here he was, standing in a corridor in Emperor Justinian's palace. It was just… just… He didn't have the words. Instead, he threw open the door and stepped inside.

There were three people in the room, all of whom he recognised.

'Ah,' said the captain, with a calm, almost bored, look on his face. 'About time too.' He was sitting on a chair, leaning back with his heels on the edge of a small bed and scratching his untidy beard.

Mud from his boots had dirtied the clean linen and his big belly bulged over the top of his military pantaloons.

'Oh dear,' Lieutenant Han said, frowning with his pointed eyebrows and wafting the air with his hand. 'Is it just me, or does he smell a bit… ripe?' he said, pointing his chin at Sanjeev. 'By the way, is your head alright? I think that murderer hit you pretty hard.'

'He's fine,' said the messenger, who had been looking out of the window too, but who was now facing Sanjeev. 'Stop mollycoddling him.'

'What…?' Sanjeev breathed, chest heaving, head a maze of thoughts, eyes darting from one face to another. A sudden thought crashed through his confusion. In panic he turned to the door. His pursuers – the palace guards! Brother Thomas! They were coming! But the door through which he had entered, the door that he had opened, had gone… *Poof!* Just like that! No door.

'Where…? How…?' Sanjeev spluttered.

'Don't worry,' the messenger said, 'no one can find us in here.'

Sanjeev nodded. His brain was refusing to make sentences and his legs had begun to wobble. 'I'm… It's… '

'You're probably wondering what's going on?' the captain said, twiddling his untidy beard.

Sanjeev nodded again.

'Well done,' said the messenger, 'you passed the challenge.'

The captain and Lieutenant Han echoed the messenger's praise, and although Sanjeev heard the words and understood their individual meanings, they, along with what he could see in front of him, made absolutely no sense whatsoever. He continued to stare at the messenger, noticing the red patch on his tunic and his wholly undamaged neck. 'But you were dead,' he finally managed to whisper. 'I saw you under the tree. Your throat was… It isn't possible. None of this is possible!' He paused. The messenger's words suddenly struck him. 'What do you mean, I've passed? Passed what?'

'Part of the test, of course!' replied Lieutenant Han. 'And what a piece of work it was too. The way you used Song Ci's ideas to catch the murderer was brilliant. A really impressive demonstration of the practical application of logic.'

They all made appreciative noises.

'Wait a minute,' Sanjeev said. 'Are you saying all of this was some kind of test? Why would you do that? Why would you put me through all that stuff?'

'We had to be sure,' replied the captain, spreading his hands. 'It's not everyone we can trust to help us. You have some special qualities, young man. You've proved that. But the journey has only just begun.'

'Only just begun? What on earth does that mean? And was the farmer really killed by the monks?'

The messenger stepped forward, a kind smile on his face. 'We can't control everything that happens in a challenge, Sanjeev.' He took hold of Sanjeev's hand. Like a magician, he passed his hand over Sanjeev's open palm. When Sanjeev looked again, he saw he was now holding a rather heavy, silvery object, shaped like a pizza slice. 'What's this?' he asked.

'Something you'll need for the trials ahead,' replied the messenger.

'For what?'

'You'll also need this,' said the captain, flourishing an object between his index finger and thumb. Coming over to Sanjeev, he dropped a key into Sanjeev's other hand. Sanjeev gasped – it was the golden monkey key!

As soon as the key landed on his palm, glints of light like sparks leaped off it. Sanjeev gawped as the forest of sparks grew thicker, and the key transformed, shifting shape until there was a little monkey in his hand with penetrating eyes looking straight into his own. But not any monkey. This one was wearing gold armour! Sanjeev was so surprised, he almost let it drop.

'Of course you'll remember this,' the captain said, referring to the key. 'It was the messenger's.'

Sanjeev nodded his head again, his eyes still on the monkey – which was now scowling at him.

'Did I tell you how he used *flies* to find the murderer?' the captain asked the others. Sanjeev watched as the captain tapped the side of his head. 'So smart!'

Sanjeev's eyes returned to the palm of his hand. He gasped. The monkey had gone and the key… was just a key. 'Who *are* you people?' he whispered.

'Oh, hardly, people!' replied Lieutenant Han. 'My name is Lu Dongbin. This,' he said, pointing to the captain, 'is Zhongli Quan. And this,' he said, pointing to the messenger, 'is Han Xiang Zi. Collectively, we are the Eight Immortals.'

'Right,' Sanjeev said. 'Sure. Fine. But… I only count three of you.'

The Immortals stared at him blankly. Sanjeev sighed. 'You're called the Eight Immortals but there are only three of you.'

'Oh, I see,' replied Han Xiang Zi. 'You'd like to know where the others are.'

'Actually, they've been… detained,' said Lu Dongbin. 'But don't worry, you'll to meet them soon enough.'

'Who's worried?' mumbled Sanjeev. But then, like a thunderbolt, a truly horrendous thought struck him. His eyes stretched wide, his throat went dry and his heart sank. 'You're… you're… Immortals?' he said, his voice hoarse.

'Yes,' replied the Han Xiang Zi.

'So, am I…' Sanjeev gulped. 'Am I dead?'

The three Immortals looked at one another… and Sanjeev had the impression they were doing their best not to laugh. This time, he felt a stab of anger.

'My dear young man,' Lu Dongbin said in an earnest tone, 'you are very much alive. And very important to us. Even as we speak, there are forces working against us. Forces you must help us defeat.'

A heavy silence fell during which the sombre faces of the Han Xiang Zi, Lu Dongbin, and Zhongli Quan regarded Sanjeev. All trace of their jocularity had gone, replaced by an urgency and seriousness that was making him feel as though burdens he hadn't accepted and knew little about were being heaped upon his shoulders. *What exactly do they expect me to do about anything? I'm not an Immortal, am I? I'm not the one with the power to send people going about their own business into the distant past.*

He was about to tell them how uncomfortable they were making him feel and how unhappy he was with…EVERYTHING THEY'D SAID AND DONE SO FAR when Han Xiang Zi shrugged. 'Well,' he said, 'I suppose we should be leaving, and I expect you want to get back to your own time and see—'

'What?' cried Sanjeev. 'You haven't told me a single thing about what's going on. One minute I'm minding my business in the Met, the next minute I've entered a time warp that I'm assuming you guys engineered, and I've been catapulted into the past to help three really strange guys steal worms from China.'

'Silkworm eggs,' Zhongli Quan corrected. 'And it's not a time warp… whatever that is.'

Sanjeev took a deep breath and started collecting all the questions he needed answers for. There were so many questions he wasn't sure where to start. This was the most mind-bending thing that had happened in the entire history of the universe, and he deserved some answers to the questions bouncing around his skull like ping-pong balls!

CHAPTER 37

—

As soon as Sanjeev opened his mouth he felt like he had stepped on black ice. His body moved in strange, uncontrollable directions, and he had become lighter than air. 'Wow!' he cried as he looked down and saw that it was true: his feet were floating above the floor. He swiped his arms, trying to clutch at the captain, who deftly stepped away. Sanjeev began flapping his arms, trying to force his body back onto the ground. It made no difference. He was still rising; he couldn't stop it.

'Help!' he cried. 'Help me!' The three Immortals watched him impassively, like scientists observing an experiment. His body was now completely horizontal, as though he were lying in a coffin, and rising even more quickly…

He slid through the ceiling as though it wasn't solid. Multi-coloured mists rose from nowhere. Twisting and turning, they swirled around him. His body began to spin around, slowly at first, but getting faster and faster. 'Get me down from here, please!' he shouted. 'Please!'

But no one did.

Once again, he was a feather in a hurricane.

'Sanjeev? Can you hear me? Sanjeev?'

Sanjeev recognised the voice. It was Mrs Milo's. Mrs Milo! A wave of happiness passed over him. He was home. He was Sanjeev in the 21st Century; not 'Boy' in 6th century Byzantium being chased by Emperor Justinian's soldiers. However, he was still horizontal, but now lying on a cold, hard floor with something soft under his head, which was… disconcerting. The mists had cleared. The hurricane had passed. And he was now subject to the laws of gravity!

He was back. He groaned, but not unhappily. That stupid, hyper-real, freaky dream had really got him going. Like a movie in ultra-fast forward, all the events of the dream replayed themselves until it got to the bit where one of those guys in that castle gave him that silvery slice of metal. A silvery slice of metal… It was only then he realised he was holding something in his hand. Something hard with sharp edges…

He opened his eyes.

'Oh, thank goodness,' Mrs Milo said.

'Are you okay, son?' A man, grey haired with a kindly face, was speaking to him. Sanjeev recognised the uniform. He was one of the Met's security guards.

'I'm fine,' Sanjeev said, still clutching the object in his hand. His mind was racing. *It can't be. It can't be that silvery slice. That would be crazy.*

'What happened?' asked Mrs Milo. 'Did you faint? Are you feeling sick?'

'I've absolutely no idea,' Sanjeev answered. The thing was, the object in his hand felt like the right shape and size. But how could it have got into his hand? It was impossible. It had all been a dream, right? Just a stupid dream.

'Do you feel nauseous, like you want to vomit?' asked the guard. 'Does your head hurt? Did you hit it?'

'No, I don't think so. My head's fine.' Sanjeev opened his hand a fraction. His heart thumped against his chest.

'Okay. Do you think you can stand up?' asked the guard.

Sanjeev got to his feet and pushed his glasses to the bridge of his nose. He was wearing glasses again! His attention zoomed back to what he was holding. He had a suspicion – a strong suspicion – about what it was, but he had to get a look at it…

'You feeling okay, champ?' asked the guard.

'I'm fine. Honestly, I'm fine.' If it was the silvery metal pizza slice, what did that mean? Did it mean the dream was real? But how could it be real? He hadn't left the Met, as far as he knew. How could he time travel and physically stay in the same place?

'He should really see a doc, just to be sure,' the guard said, addressing Mrs Milo. 'He can sit in the staff canteen and we can keep an eye on him there. That all right with you, champ? Maybe have somethin' to eat too? Maybe you got low blood sugar? A hot drink and some food might help.'

Sanjeev nodded. The guard looked away. Sanjeev, watching the man from the corner of his eye, opened his hand a fraction and peeked at what it held. He gasped. The silvery slice.

So... It wasn't a dream? But... But... His mind reeled. He'd come to the museum and looked at the Byzantine mosaic and somehow it had transported him back to the 6th century? That was crazy! What for? Just to get a piece of pizza-shaped metal? That made no sense! In his mind's eye, he also saw the little gold key being dropped into his hand too... Now he thought about it, he could feel a chain around his neck, and something dangling from it.

'Alright,' said the guard, 'the staff canteen's along the hall. Let's take a walk there, shall we?'

Sanjeev nodded again. With his other hand, he pressed his fingers through his top, to feel the small, cold object on the chain. The small, cold, *key-shaped* object. 'Oh!' he said. The guard and Mrs Milo turned and peered anxiously into his face. 'I'm fine,' he said quickly.

'Are we walkin' too fast for ya, champ?' asked the guard. 'How about a little fresh air first?'

But Sanjeev never got to hear the rest of the guard's suggestion because the guard's radio suddenly burst into life. The guard put it to his ear. Sanjeev and Mrs Milo watched as the guard replied and

put the radio away again. He was standing with his mouth open.
'Oh my goodness,' the guard said.

'What is it? What's happening?' asked Sanjeev.

'There's been a theft, just a few streets away. A Met security
truck's been robbed.'

PART 6

NEW YORK CITY ⊢

THE PRESENT DAY

CHAPTER 38

—

Ted Danton took off his cap, looked up at the sky, and scratched his head. The sky, nearly as grey as the city, was crisp with winter. The newscaster had talked about some weather coming in, low pressure in the east. Ted sniffed the air. It was clear now, but a storm was on its way, no doubt about it. And with it, a possibility of strong winds, maybe even sleet. Not for a few hours, but it'd get a bit rough before then. He watched his breath condense in front of him. *Not a day for a tour*, he thought. *Not in this weather.* Not unless you're being offered five times the usual fare, as he was. He looked at the sky again, put his cap back on. *The weather should hold today, but tomorrow's going to be a doozy.*

The time was 12:45pm, and Ted was at the Downtown Manhattan Heliport, waiting to pick up his only tour group of the day. It was a route he'd taken countless times over the last seventeen years: take off from his base at Pier 10 at the bottom of Manhattan, do a circle around the Upper Bay and Lady Liberty before heading uptown to Central Park, then return to base. It never got boring though, there was always something along the way that had escaped his notice until that flight. Today, however, he wanted to get it over with quickly, get back to his wife, Jill and daughter, Lee. Then bury himself under a blanket, turn on the TV, and ignore the sleet crashing against the windows.

But that would have to wait. Today would be a bit different – a privately booked tour for three people who wouldn't listen when Ted suggested they fly out an hour earlier to avoid the bad weather.

A black limo pulled up. *Nice ride,* thought Ted. The front passenger door opened and a man in a well-tailored black suit got out. He fastened a button on his suit and opened the rear door. A thin, old man dressed in a grey suit that matched his hair climbed out of the car and straightened himself. Ted looked at him, puzzled. The man looked about seventy, and yet somehow not... Two other men walked either side of the old man, whose eyes stayed locked on Ted's. He had had an excellent late lunch, but suddenly Ted felt lightheaded and a throbbing pain started at the back of his skull.

'Good afternoon, gentlemen, and welcome to Ted's Tours,' Ted said, smiling his broadest, customer-friendly smile and extending a hand to the elderly man despite the increasing headache. 'You must be Mr Chan.'

'Yes. I am Chan,' he said, shaking Ted's hand. He gestured to the men behind him. 'And these are my associates, Mr Yang Chee and Mr An Ho.'

'My pleasure,' Ted said, turning and nodding at the men. Yang had lanky hair and was skinny; An was the opposite, looking like he was made of concrete. 'How are you doin' today, guys?'

An Ho's face – as hard as granite – and small, suspicious eyes lost in deep sockets stared back at Ted while Yang brushed a stray hair away from his face, keeping his thin-lipped mouth closed. Ted waited a moment more for the men to speak but neither did. It made Ted feel uncomfortable, so he launched into his opening speech, one he knew so well he could repeat it in his sleep. 'New York City. The Big Apple. The City That Never Sleeps. Today you're going to see it in a way you've never dreamed possible.

'At the moment, we've got some exceptional visibility, so prepare yourself for some awesome sights. And maybe,' he said, looking at the eastern sky, 'a bit later, some adventure.'

Ted reached back and gave the bright red helicopter a pat on the side, as one would pat a horse's neck. 'Today, you'll be flying in an AS350 NP. Twin engines, enhanced manoeuvrability and performance. Good enough for the police. This one here's been my baby for the last thirteen years and boy does she know how to move. I named her Helen, after my—'

'That is all very interesting, Mr Danton,' Chan said, looking at his wristwatch, 'but wouldn't it be better if we were on our way?'

'Sure thing, Mr Chan. I'm sorry, but before we board, I've got a couple of formalities to take care of.' He opened the door to the copter and removed a clipboard lying on the pilot's seat. 'If you wouldn't mind signing this waiver, here,' he said and marked an X on one of the lines, 'and here.' He handed the clipboard to the old man who passed it on to An Ho without even glancing at it.

'It's to show that I've told you all the safety features,' Ted said. Silently, An Ho signed the form and passed it back.

'Oh, and one last thing before we take-off,' Ted said, removing a wand-shaped object from the cab of the copter. 'It's a routine precaution'. He moved toward one of the men, the metal detector held out in front of him.

'That will not be necessary,' Chan said, the edge in his voice stopping Ted dead in his tracks. Ted opened his mouth to speak, but Chan spoke first, softer now. 'I assure you, everything has been confirmed in advance. And I would very much like to get in the air before the weather threatens to cut our tour short.'

'Like I said, sir, a formality,' Ted said and put the detector back in the cabin. 'What home base doesn't know won't hurt them, right?' He opened the door and welcomed them inside. 'If you are ready,' he said.

Mr Yang got in first, climbing into the furthest seat in the back. Ted continued to hold the door.

'Mr An would like to sit in the passenger seat up front, Mr Danton,' Chan explained. 'I am sure you will not mind.' Mr An did not wait for a reply but began walking around the copter.

'Sure...' Ted said.

Chan paused before climbing into the helicopter and taking seat behind the pilot's chair.

A few moments later, they were ready for take-off.

Chapter 39

—

Ted revved the motor and they lifted away, out over the East River piers and into the sky. His headache was better now. He turned up the heater in the helicopter, flipped on the wipers to clear the windscreen. Then he adjusted the mouthpiece of his microphone. As usual, the noise in the cabin from the engine and blades was deafening and he and the passengers were wearing microphones and headphones in order to hear one another speak. 'Have you folks been to the city before?' Ted asked, looking into the mirrors he'd had installed to better be able to speak with his back-seat passengers. The two men were looking out the windows and barely took notice of the fact he'd spoken.

Chan appeared to be the only one capable of speech. 'Yes, we have,' he said.

'Well, you probably haven't seen her like this.' Ted pointed out his window. 'Below us to the north, you'll see the Brooklyn Bridge. A real beauty, isn't she? Oldest suspension bridge in the United States, built in 1883.' He looked out over Brooklyn, thinking of Jill – who was originally from there – and Lee. *Be home soon,* he thought.

Ted, grinning at a memory of Jill teaching Lee to bake and both of them covered in flour, glimpsed Chan's eyes. Startled, he blinked hard and turning away, refocused on steering the helicopter. He pulled on the cyclic stick and the helicopter made a wide turn, away from the sullen clouds coming in from the east. It had been the way Chan had stared – and his expression, sort of intrigued… knowing.

It was as if he saw right through me. Ted fought down the feeling that something wasn't right as the helicopter continued towards the centre of the harbour.

'That there's Governors Island, first called The Island of Nuts, not because of the people on it but because of the nut trees,' Ted said, but none of them seemed the least bit interested. Chan was looking at his watch.

'How fast are we going?' he asked.

'One hundred knots, Mr Chan,' Ted said, not meeting his eyes.

'And how fast can the machine go?'

Ted smiled. 'Most AS350s do about one hundred and twenty knots, but Helen here, well, I've had her up at one-forty.'

'I would like to see Central Park at 1:50pm. I have heard there is to be a display that I do not want to miss,' Chan said. 'First, however, I am interested in seeing Columbia University from the air. I know someone who goes there.'

'Yes, sir. I'll make sure we get there on time, safe and sound,' Ted said. *Columbia University?* he thought. That was an unusual request. *Okay, whatever. You're the one that's footing the bill.*

The Statue of Liberty was coming into view. 'And there she is, our Lady Liberty. Over ninety metres from the ground to the tip of her torch. I'll circle around the crown so you get a good look at her face. Sure looks pretty with that dusting of snow on her. Feel free to take photos.'

The red copter caught the attention of the tourists inside the great statue. Ted took them close enough to see the kids pointing out at them, waving their hands hello.

'Here's something most people don't know,' Ted said. 'The crown has seven rays of light emanating from it in the form of a halo. They were supposed to represent the seven continents, the seven seas. Along with her torch, Liberty was supposed to shine over the entire world.'

Ted looked at his passengers. Chan, An and Yang hadn't budged. No cameras, no talk, nothing. *Weird*, Ted thought. *Everyone takes pictures.*

They left the Statue of Liberty and continued on, Ted saying a few words about Ellis Island, and a bit more about the One World Trade Centre, which usually started up discussions about the Twin Towers, but not today. When they turned north to head uptown to view skyscrapers like the Chrysler, Met Life and Empire State buildings, he decided perhaps they didn't want to hear him speak at all.

The sky had grown darker. They headed up the West Side, passing the flight in silence until they were hovering over the university. 'There you go, Mr Chan. Columbia University,' Ted said, glancing in his mirror.

Chan was looking at his watch again. 'Ah yes,' he said, without lifting his head. Ted looked at his own. 1:42pm. Central Park was close now, but they'd have to put on a bit of speed to get there early. He turned sharply, changed the setting on the throttle, and headed east once more.

For the first time since they had taken to the air, An Ho, who had been so motionless in the passenger seat that Ted thought he was asleep, unbuckled his seat belt.

'Please, sir,' Ted said, 'you must keep your belt on for the entire duration of the trip. Company policy.'

An Ho, ignoring him, bent down to look under the control panel. Ted watched as the man reached into his pocket and took out a screwdriver. *What?!*

'I don't know what you're doing, sir, but I must insist that—'

Through his uniform, Ted felt something hard and metal press against his side. He knew what it was: the barrel of a gun.

'You seem like a reasonably smart man, Mr Danton. A practical man.' Chan, who was holding the gun, did not appear to be shouting, but everything he said came through clearly.

'I am going to give you instructions. These may surprise you, but I assure you I am not kidding.' The barrel of the gun dug deeper into his side.

'We will be changing our flight plans somewhat,' Chan continued. And as Chan related their new coordinates, Ted listened almost with disbelief. He had started kicking himself for not taking all the safety precautions when Chan said something that made his blood turn cold.

'If you have any regard for self-preservation and the safety of Jill and Lee,' Chan said, with another prod of the gun, 'you will do exactly what we say. To the letter.'

Chapter 40

—

Ted turned the headset back on and adjusted the mic. *I could alert Ground Control and they'd never know*, he thought. *Code 7500 – hijack.* He tried to work out the possibilities but everything was moving too fast.

'I believe the code is *not* 7500…' Chan said, his voice as flat as iron.

Ted gawked at him.

Chan gave an icy smile. 'For an engine-related emergency, the correct one is 7700,' he said and motioned towards the radio.

Ted reached forwards and flipped a switch on the radio with a trembling hand. He felt his throat tighten.

Over the din of the motor and blades came a wash of static topped with a piercing hum. Ted quickly adjusted the knobs until the channel was clear.

'Ground Control here. Name and location,' came a thin voice.

'N352LH. That's November three five two, Lima, Hotel. Danton calling.'

'Roger. What appears to be the problem, Danton?'

'We've got a 7700 – engine trouble. Rotors not responding.' Ted thought of the gun and fought to keep any emotion out of his voice, anything that might make Ground Control suspicious. '45H, level nine hundred forty.'

'Say heading,' the box demanded.

'I'm going to try to make it to North Woods. Don't know if there are any helipads around here – might have to land her on the roof of a building if things get worse.' Ted looked in the mirror. Chan was looking in the mirror as well, watching Ted to make sure he didn't try anything funny.

They heard the controller shout to the others in his office, 'Need all the help you can give me. Got a 7700!' He addressed Danton again, his voice calmer. 'You stay right there, Danton. We'll talk you through every step.'

'Roger. Wilco,' Ted said.

Chan gestured with the barrel of the gun at the radio. 'Off!'

Ted's eyebrows rose. If he switched the radio off, Ground Control would wonder why he wasn't responding. Chan's gun twitched again. Ted switched the radio off.

'Now,' Chan said. 'I have told you exactly what to do. Do it right... I will not suffer mistakes.'

Ted, his hands gripping the cyclic stick tightly, braced himself for the steep descent they'd forced upon him. The rotor blades twisted above them, assuming an angle that wouldn't hold them aloft for long.

'Hold on!' he shouted. They lurched to the right. Ted stomped on the left foot pedal and released it quickly for fear he'd send them into a tailspin. All of his training had been to help him fight these emergency conditions, not simulate them. He pulled back on the throttle, then pumped it to give the impression that the engine was cutting out. The helicopter was weaving erratically now, losing altitude rapidly, barely in his control. He felt like a kite buffeted by the wind; the skyscrapers crowded together as if they were great trees reaching out to him. Ted's knuckles grew white as he gripped the cyclic stick. The chopper was rattling violently, and he wasn't sure he could hold her together.

In an instant, Central Park spread before them. He pulled the cyclic stick once again, and the helicopter yawed left, out towards the Met and the Great Lawn Oval.

'There!' Chan shouted, pointing to the far end of the lawn. They were just above the trees now, coming in fast. 'Show's over! You will land softly,' Chan said.

Softly? Ted thought to himself. *We'll be lucky to walk out of this!*

He quickly adjusted the rotors, gave it some extra throttle to stabilise it. The helicopter wobbled awkwardly, clumsily hovering above the snow-covered field for a few seconds before landing heavily.

After a moment, Yang spoke up. 'I don't see them, boss.'

Chan straightened out the wrinkles in his suit. 'If they have failed me, they will join their ancestors in Hell,' he said.

CHAPTER 41

—

No sooner had the helicopter touched down when a van came screeching around the Great Lawn Oval road from the east. It seemed to Ted that the driver had lost control of the vehicle. His jaw fell open as a second later it was on the field, carving deep tracks in the snow as it charged towards them. The van braked hard and came to a sharp halt just outside the reach of the copter's rotors. The doors to the van opened and three large men jumped out. Two went around and opened the van's rear doors, then began tugging on something inside. It looked like an oversized crate, shaped like a large coffin. As soon as it was partway out, the third man grabbed a handle on the side. A fourth came from inside the van and joined them. Ducking their heads low, they raced toward the chopper.

Ted saw the flashing lights of the police cars between the trees before he heard the sirens.

The barrel of the gun pressed against his ribs more firmly. A voice came from close behind his ear. 'Remember, do exactly as we tell you and you might live.'

The door to the helicopter was flung open. The men with the crate were almost at the door. By now, three patrol cars were racing toward them. One man jumped into the helicopter, and with as much care as possible, guided the large crate into the back.

Ted heard gunfire. He jumped in surprise, wondering if he'd been shot. He turned his head as far as he dared to one side, and saw one of the men in the cab firing at the oncoming police cars. Chan,

An Ho and Yang had all jumped out of the helicopter to help with the loading of the crate, but were periodically turning to shoot the automatic weapons they had been concealing.

The police had made an arc, turning the sides of the patrol cars toward the van. The officers got out, and using the cars as shields, returned fire. Ted cowered, sinking deeper in his seat for cover. The police officers were fifty metres away, but every shot rang as if they were right next to the copter.

A cry next to him made him jump. 'Get up!' An Ho shouted, his gun pointed at Ted's chest. Ted unbuckled himself and slowly raised his hands above his head. An Ho gestured with the muzzle of his gun toward the door. Chan's accomplices were still firing a semi-automatic machine gun; the police were taking a moment to reload and consider their options. Another car screeched up between the van and helicopter. Now that the crate was safe in the helicopter, the men who had brought the crate made a break for the getaway car, firing their guns as they ran close to the ground.

An Ho fired another volley and grabbed Ted, heaving him out of the helicopter. Ted raised his arms higher, expecting he would be used as a hostage. Instead, cradling the machine gun in one arm, An Ho threw Ted to the ground. Yang, standing next to An Ho, raised the barrel of his gun and levelled it at Ted's head. Ted raised his hands. 'No, please!' he yelled, his voice almost lost in the barrage of shots being fired back and forth.

'Leave him!'

Ted opened his eyes. It was Chan. He had given the order to Yang and Yang was lowering his weapon.

'Get in! Let's go!' Chan cried. Then, leaning down and pressing his face so close to Ted's ear, Ted could feel his hot breath, Chan whispered to him.

With the gunfire still raging around him, Ted tried to forget the pain and flatten himself against the cold earth, watching as Chan's accomplices in the getaway car pull away into the distance, bullets puncturing the boot, and feeling the blast of air as helicopter rotors engaged and spun faster and faster. He laid his head down on the cold, snowy grass. The helicopter rose into the air and, nose down, zoomed across the park, gaining altitude all the time. There was nothing Ted could do but watch… and wonder.

Chan had spared him. He was a witness, yet they had not killed him. It didn't make sense. But then, neither did Chan's whispered words: 'Her name was Lee, too.'

CHAPTER 42

The police helipad on 57th Street, was, as Chan suspected, able to get a chopper in the air two minutes after receiving the incoming alert from the NYPD. Chan twisted a dial on the hand-held radio he was holding to better listen in to the police channel. Two men were in the police chopper – Johnson the pilot and Wilkes, a crack-shot sniper. Chan smiled. He hadn't expected that. A line of communication to the ground troops had also been opened so the officers would be able to track the copter's coordinates and follow in patrol cars.

For a couple of moments, there was only static, then, 'Five fifty-four, here. We've spotted them, Captain, and are in pursuit. Perps flying a red Star helicopter, model AS350, N352LH, at an altitude of 1,500 feet, headed north by north-west, toward the docks. I think they may be looking to make a break for it over the East River.'

'Follow and await support. Immediately. Proceed with caution. Repeat, proceed with caution. Perps armed and dangerous.'

Inside the cockpit, An Ho was busy. Not only did he have to avoid the skyscrapers that threatened to knock them from the sky at every turn, but he also had to make sure they weren't in range of the sniper. And all the while, Yang was tinkering with the underside of the dashboard.

Yang was lying on his back, the metal panel he'd removed at his side. His left hand was lost inside the wiring, his right held a pair of wire clippers. He was about to reach in with the clippers when An Ho swerved sharply, nearly grazing a series of balconies.

'Steady there, An Ho. I would like to cut the right wire,' Yang said.

'I will see what I can do to help,' An Ho replied.

They levelled off and Yang made a quick grab inside with the clippers. He dropped the clippers and pulled out the severed ends of the wires. Holding these in one hand, he reached with his other to the inner pocket of his suit and removed an electronic box the size of a mobile phone. Two screw terminals stuck out of one end. Still on his back, Yang attached one end of the wire to each of the terminals, took out a roll of black electrical tape from his pocket, and sealed the wires in place. He paused as the helicopter went into a roll and then taped the box up against the control board.

'Done,' he said and sat back in the passenger seat.

'Got it,' An Ho grunted.

As soon as he could, he made three very rapid moves around buildings, so they were facing in the opposite direction from which they'd come. Up ahead loomed the MetLife building. While Yang kept watch, An Ho sped towards the building – not only towards it, but at it – so close, it seemed as if they were planning to crash into it head on. Suddenly a section of the building appeared to move. A metal screen – complete with two rows of fake windows – slid up like a giant garage door, revealing a two-storey section of gutted office space inside the building: a hangar thirty floors in the air.

The helicopter entered as gracefully as a hummingbird sidling up to a flower. An instant after it was in, the screen lowered down behind it.

'We've… lost them, sir,' Johnson said, the frustration in his voice coming through loud and clear.

Chan smiled, still listening in as he strode away from the helicopter.

'You what? You lost a red copter?'

Another call came in, this time from ground support – updated info on the shootout at the museum. The escape vehicle was racing towards midtown on 5th Avenue. One officer had been shot and was en route to the hospital in critical condition, along with the pilot of the hijacked chopper, who appeared to be in shock but okay. They had also identified the stolen object: a jade suit from the Han Dynasty.

'Johnson, whatcha got?'

'Nothing yet, Captain.'

'Stay in position and keep your eyes peeled. They must've gone somewhere.'

'Affirmative,' Johnson replied.

Inside the makeshift hangar, Yang checked the box he had attached to the helicopter's instrument panel was securely taped. Then, before leaving the cockpit himself, he pressed a button on the side of the box. A green light began blinking. He got out and walked to the open space where the skyscraper windows had been. Nearby, a small table held a pair of binoculars. He picked them up and scanned the sky. After a few moments, Yang spotted the chopper that had been following them.

'They're coming,' he said to Chan, who nodded.

Meanwhile, a group of men had removed the crate from inside the red helicopter. They carried it over to where Chan and An Ho stood – beside a large grey helicopter with *Bai Lu* written on its side in gold. They opened the hatch and loaded the crate with the jade suit inside. Once the crate was strapped in place, the men got out and grabbed four mannequins, one dressed in a pilot's uniform, two in black suits, one in white. These they ran back to the red chopper. One of the men gave a loud whistle once the mannequins were in place.

Yang picked up the drone controller that sat on the table, depressed a lever, and started the rotors of the helicopter. He eased

THE GOLD MONKEY KEY ~ 177

the chopper up slowly so it hovered off the floor and sent it back out of the hangar. As soon as the chopper had cleared the edge of the building, the screen that had camouflaged the entrance rolled back down.

An Ho took his position in the cockpit of the grey helicopter, with the crate and Yang behind him. Chan, sitting beside An Ho in the cabin with the hand-held radio on his lap, looked at his watch. It had all taken three minutes. Perfect.

'Wait!' he heard the voice on the radio say. 'There they are! They've changed direction and are heading west.'

'Stay on them, Johnson. Do not fire unless fired upon. Await my command. Repeat, await my command.'

In his mind, Chan imagined Johnson keeping an eye on the red chopper, looking for a chance at a shot. 'The chopper seems to be experiencing engine problems – it is bobbing up and down erratically,' Johnson said. Then he added, 'Almost within range for a shot, Captain. Awaiting your command. Still heading west. Chopper destabilised. Listing hard to right. Smoke trailing from the engine case. Suspect imminent touchdown.'

Chan nodded, and Yang pressed a button on the controller. Inside the hangar, the sound of the explosion sounded like a distant firework.

Johnson's voice came over the radio again. 'She's gone, Captain. Blew up somewhere out over the Hudson River. No chance of survivors. Better send officers in to help with falling debris.'

Over the airwaves, there came a long sigh. 'Good work, Johnson. Do a flyby to confirm status of hijacked chopper and then report back. I want you on the ground before that storm hits.'

'Roger, Captain.'

A few moments later, not a word was said as the building's screen was raised again, and An Ho flew the three of them and the jade suit into the oncoming snow storm.

PART 7

NEW YORK AND HOBOKEN ⊷ THE PRESENT DAY

CHAPTER 43

━

While the police cordoned off the area and made sure that it was safe for those in the Met to leave, Sanjeev, Anton, Basem and Jermaine listened to and immediately relayed every wild rumour there was about the robbery.

Some said the thieves had stolen the Temple of Dendur, which was preposterous, they decided, because it was massive and probably weighed, like, a thousand tonnes and wouldn't fit in the back of a truck. Others said it was King Henry VIII of England's armour. That didn't seem so impossible, but who needed some fat king's clothes? Then Anton had said he'd heard it was a massive painting called 'Washington Crossing the Delaware' and that it was worth a billion dollars at least, which they agreed was an excellent reason to steal it – even if they couldn't figure out how the thieves would get it out of New York without having a million cop cars chasing them.

In the end, it was Mrs Milo who told them what the stolen item was. Thieves had held up a security truck outside the Met. It had been coming from JFK to the Met to deliver part of a special exhibition from China – a 2,500-year-old artefact, designed to be worn like a suit of clothes, but made completely of jade.

'How much is it worth?' had been Anton's first question. 'What's jade?' was his second, and 'How did the robbers escape?' was his third.

Mrs Milo answered the first two questions patiently, but she had no idea how the thieves had escaped. Anton pulled a face, but then he realised he had a good signal on his phone. While everyone waited for the doors to be reopened, he trawled social media, where pictures of a helicopter landing illegally in Central Park had gone viral, along with men carrying what looked like a body-sized crate!

'Okay, everyone,' said a booming voice, silencing the chatter in the Great Hall where people were waiting, and tearing the four boys' attention away from Anton's phone. 'We would like to thank you all for your co-operation today. You've all been very patient. The good news is the police department has advised us that the area is now safe and you are all free to go.'

A loud 'Hurray!' and some clapping followed, then the tall front doors of the Met were quickly swung back, and people began pouring through them and down the stone steps towards the street. 'Freedom!' cried Anton, which got a laugh.

Through the open doors, Sanjeev could see the red tail-lights of cabs as they made their way up 5th Avenue. It was now after 4pm. The school had called his mother and father, so he wasn't worried about that, but he did want to know if his father had managed to put up the posters: when he'd looked at his mobile, he'd seen that the screen was cracked and blank. He must have landed on it when he hit the ground. Had someone found his dog? The thought of Jigsaw on the streets, wandering cold, hungry and lost made Sanjeev's stomach sink.

When it was their turn to pass through the doors, the four boys stepped into the late afternoon and gasped. The outside air was freezing – so cold it burned their lungs. Anton huffed and blew huge white clouds. Jermaine and Basem did the same. Sanjeev felt that his nose was ready to fall off. He slipped on his hand-knitted gloves, ignoring Anton's smirk.

'Man, it's cold!' Sanjeev complained, wrapping his arms around his body and pulling his coat tightly to him.

'Anton looks like a Wamajamer!' yelled Jermaine as they clattered down the stone steps towards Mrs Milo, who was shepherding students from Class 8 to the side and counting to make sure everyone was there. Sanjeev, Jermaine and Basem laughed. Anton, who couldn't think of another ice creature's name from *Planet Odyssey* to call Jermaine, settled instead on shoving him.

'Right,' called Mrs Milo, giving Anton one of her famous, icy stares for his shoving Jermaine, but looking too cold to stop and admonish him, 'we'll go back the same way we came. There's a bus waiting for us at Hoboken that'll take you all home. Any questions? No? Good, so let's get going. And stay together.'

With Mrs Milo in the lead, the class trudged along 5th Avenue. Sanjeev, head down, shivering, was walking as quickly as he could – they all were.

As he walked, Sanjeev thought back on all that had happened since he had arrived at the Met: the snowball on the side of the head, the Silk Road exhibition, the mosaic, the crazy… He didn't know what to call it – episode? The three brothers, the Eight Immortals, the theft, the silvery slice, the gold key… He felt the slice in his pocket, and then it hit him.

'Oh no!' he whispered, as he dug his hands as far as they would go into his coat's pockets. He delved into the coat's inside pockets, checked the pockets of his jeans – front and back. It wasn't there. He'd lost it. He'd lost the yellow duck, Jigsaw's favourite toy. He groaned. *Could things get any worse?*

CHAPTER 44

━

The journey back to Hoboken seemed to take forever. On the subway journey, the feeling of panic he had experienced on the way to the Met had not returned. He wasn't sure why it hadn't, but he was glad. When they got to 33rd Street, they saw the packed station. Sure enough, the PATH train out of New York City was full to overflowing too: men and women in smart clothes carrying briefcases, students with backpacks, a few men in dusty overalls. Some read newspapers or texted, but many were talking to their neighbours about the robbery at the Met.

Like the rest of Class 8, Sanjeev had grabbed a strap that hung from the carriage's ceiling when he entered the train, so now, as the train twisted this way and that and hammered noisily along the tracks, he swung back and forth, covertly surveying all the people sitting or standing near him. But he soon grew bored and instead stared out of the windows, though there was little to see except darkness, and his face reflected in the glass, staring back. He looked at his face. It was a face, he thought, that didn't belong to someone who had an incredible story to tell, one that no one in that train would believe – not even his friends. He told himself he looked like a regular sort of fourteen-year-old. Regular nose, regular eyes, regular glasses, regular – he flattened down some wayward strands – hair. And yet…

He turned to his left where Basem, Anton and Jermaine were standing further up the train. Anton, who seemed to sense Sanjeev glancing at him, raised his head, grinned, then looked down again and continued playing something on his mobile. *Breakneck*, Sanjeev suspected. Sanjeev dropped his gaze and stared at his feet. He wondered where he had dropped Jigsaw's favourite toy. It could have been anywhere, he told himself. An image of Jigsaw standing on an icy street corner made his throat tighten. Was he ever going to see him again? Maybe they should check the dog pound one more time? The guy there had said to check back in a couple of days. When he got home, he would ask his father to take him there.

Sanjeev realised that while he had been thinking about Jigsaw, his fingers had closed around the gold key on the chain around his neck. It was strange that Anton hadn't said anything about it. He had expected Anton to give him a hard time about the fact that he was wearing a necklace! The pizza slice piece of metal he had also been given was in his jacket pocket, safely buttoned up there. He didn't want to take it out in the middle of the train carriage. Instead, he would look at it more closely later when there were fewer prying eyes. Nevertheless, they were both part of the same crazy story. And what was that story? He still didn't know what to think. Making more sense of it would have to wait till later too.

'Class 8! We're coming into our station soon,' called Mrs Milo, shouting above the noise of the train with ease. 'Make sure you've got everything!'

Behind Mrs Milo, Sanjeev caught Anton silently mimicking Mrs Milo's words. Jermaine and Basem were ready to burst. Sanjeev shook his head. Trust Anton. A few minutes later, the train pulled into the station and a whole bunch of people got off. Mrs Milo quickly gathered Class 8 together and, leading from the front, marched them down the platform towards the exit. Outside the station, she spied their bus. 'Over there,' she yelled. 'Let's go.' Sanjeev was walking next to Anton when he suddenly froze.

'Did you hear that?' he said, clutching Anton's arm and pulling him to a standstill.

'Hear what?'

Sanjeev didn't answer. Instead, he turned his head left and right, searching out the direction of the noise.

Still sat on the ground was the woman he had seen earlier with the cardboard sign that said, *Lost my job. Lost my home. Lost my family.* She was leaning against the station wall and in the palm of her hand she was holding the squeaky yellow duck. She slowly squeezed it again.

'You found it!' cried Sanjeev, rushing over.

'Sure did,' the woman replied. 'You dropped it when your buddy hit ya with the snowball. Nice shot, by the way,' she said to Anton.

Anton nodded, obviously pleased.

'So,' continued the woman, 'whose toy is this?'

'It's my dog's.'

'That makes sense,' the woman said as a shape moved under the blanket next to her. As she spoke, the woman's hand reached out and dragged the blanket away to reveal a dog – with a black eye patch of fur, with one ear up, one down.

'Jigsaw!' Sanjeev yelled as Jigsaw's snout poked out from beneath the blanket. For a second, Jigsaw didn't move. He stared up at Sanjeev. But then Sanjeev cried Jigsaw's name again, and the spell broke. Scrambling madly, Jigsaw launched himself at Sanjeev, his tail revolving like the rotors on a helicopter as he circled and re-circled Sanjeev's legs.

'Where have you been?' cried Sanjeev as Jigsaw whined and whirled in delight. 'I've been looking everywhere for you!' The strangest day of his life had suddenly become the best ever. 'This is amazing. Thank you so much for looking after him...' Sanjeev said.

The woman smiled. 'You're most welcome.'

'How did you find him?' Sanjeev managed to ask as Jigsaw tried to lick his face off.

'Well, I was messing around with the toy when your dog went by. Soon as he heard it, he seemed real interested. With his collar and all, I knew he belonged to somebody, and I guessed you were carrying the toy for a reason…' The woman shrugged. 'Saw there was a number on the collar. Wanted to call it, but…' She motioned towards the empty plate next to the sign. 'Ain't got no money. So, all I could do was ask him to stay here. And he's been keepin' me mighty fine company all this time.'

'Boys! Let's go.' It was Mrs Milo calling.

'We've gotta go,' said Sanjeev. 'Will you be here tomorrow?' he called as he, Anton and Jigsaw turned and started to run towards Mrs Milo, whose eyebrows had risen and whose mouth was getting ready to shout something about not bringing that dog on the bus.

The woman shrugged. 'Well, I won't say I won't, and I won't say I will cause I just don't know.'

Sanjeev explained about Jigsaw's being missing for so long, and eventually Mrs Milo allowed him on the bus home. Jigsaw was skinny, his bones stuck out and his face was lean, but he was happy.

As soon as Sanjeev arrived home, his mother squealed in surprise, and Jigsaw jumped out of Sanjeev's arms. Amazingly, Sanjeev's mother swept Jigsaw up and even allowed him to lick her face!

'How did you find him? Where was he?' his mother cried.

'A woman at the station found him. She knew he was mine. She kept him for me.'

'Really? Which person?'

Sanjeev shrugged. 'I dunno. She had a sign in red crayon.'

'I've got to tell your father what's happened,' she said and ran to the telephone.

In fact, his father was in a meeting, so Sanjeev's mother left a message. He would get the good news soon enough.

'He's looking skinny,' his mother commented when she returned. 'I don't think that will last long.'

They both laughed. In the short space of time he had been home, Jigsaw had eaten nearly two cans of dog food, three special treats, and half a dozen doggie chocolates. After all of that, there was only one more thing for him to do: sleep. Sanjeev watched him for a while as he dozed contentedly in his basket.

'Mom?' Sanjeev said.

'Mmmm?' his mother replied, continuing to make notes from an enormous art book she was reading.

'You know I said at breakfast I would tell you something?'

'Yes, I remember,' his mother replied absentmindedly.

Sanjeev took a deep breath. 'What I wanted to say was… it was me. I left the gate open. That's how Jigsaw escaped. It was my fault.'

His mother looked up from her book and gazed at him in silence. 'Are you sure, my love?' she asked, facing him.

'Yes.'

'Your father was worried it was his fault.'

Sanjeev looked down. 'I know, I should have said something.'

'So how do you know it was you to blame?' his mother asked.

'I was the last one out of the gate. Dad had already left by then.'

His mother closed the book gently. 'Look,' she said, 'we all make mistakes. But if we're lucky, we get to learn from them.'

'I know, but…' Sanjeev couldn't finish his sentence. He felt choked.

'Listen. You know you made a mistake. You've admitted that, right?'

Sanjeev nodded.

'Well, it takes guts to do that. And you'll be more careful next time, right?'

Sanjeev nodded again.

'Good. So off you go. Let me finish making these notes for my lecture and we can talk more about it later, if you want.'

CHAPTER 45

—

Upstairs, with his bedroom door closed behind him, Sanjeev sat on his bed and looked at the silvery slice and the gold monkey key. Finding Jigsaw again had almost pushed all the things that had happened in the Met out of his head.

Almost, but not quite.

He touched the silvery slice, felt its cold metal, the embossed figure on it. If the whole Byzantium thing was a dream, how had he got the silvery thing and the key? And if Byzantium hadn't been a dream… what was it? Nothing made sense.

He picked up the slice and looked at it more closely. On one side of it, there was something that might be a rabbit, but he wasn't sure. It had enormous ears, so perhaps it was a hare. It was definitely beautiful. The animal's legs ran along the rounded edge of the slice, but its ears pointed inwards, towards the slice's narrow end. Sanjeev estimated he had about a third of the total object – if it was circular, which he thought it was.

A memory flashed through his mind. The thing in Bryant Park – three rabbits in the middle of New York City that had been there one minute and gone the next.

Just then, Jigsaw pranced in, sat down beside him, and sniffed his hand. Sanjeev gave Jigsaw a pat and looked at the key, peering deeply into the unmoving figure's eyes. *A key to what?* he wondered.

Jigsaw moved a little closer and gazed up at him, his brown, liquid eyes watching intently.

Would it come alive and turn into the monkey in the gold armour again? Sanjeev wondered. He held his arm out straight with the key on his palm. Jigsaw's tail began wagging faster. Sanjeev breathed deeply, focusing on the key and willing the monkey to reappear. Suddenly, Jigsaw raised his paw and plopped it on Sanjeev's arm. The key bounced off Sanjeev's hand and toppled onto floor. As Sanjeev reached for it, Jigsaw, still sitting, dropped his nose to the floor and began sniffing, his head moving side to side. Two or three times, his nose passed over the key, but he didn't stop. It was like he hadn't seen it.

Puzzled, Sanjeev pointed to it. Jigsaw put his nose next to where Sanjeev's finger was. Again, it was as though the key wasn't there. Sanjeev picked up the key and tossed it into the air. Jigsaw's eyes remained on Sanjeev's hands. Sanjeev caught the key and dropped it onto the floor. Jigsaw's eyes didn't move away from Sanjeev's face.

'Weird,' Sanjeev whispered. The key didn't seem like it was going to change into the monkey in the armour, and it also seemed like it was invisible. Sanjeev picked it up. Now he was really concerned. If no one but him could see and feel the key and pizza slice, was he going insane? Was he imagining objects that didn't really exist?

Thinking the game was over, Jigsaw bounced to his feet and pushed his face into Sanjeev's hand. As Sanjeev tickled Jigsaw's ears, the slow realisation that he'd seen a monkey in armour somewhere before crept over him. He looked over at his computer… and froze. Where were the cracks on the screen, the ones that had run across it like jagged rivers, the ones made by the boy when he tried to break through it?

Leaving the silver slice on his bed, he stood next to the laptop, and reaching out, he gingerly touched the screen and dragged his fingers down it, watching as his fingertips glided over the seamlessly smooth surface. It had definitely been cracked. The boy had shoved against it, and it had cracked!

He sank onto his computer chair and held his head in his hands. Maybe it wasn't the screen that was cracked. Maybe it was him! Maybe he should tell someone about all of this? Maybe he should speak to…

He looked up. The CPU was making a funny, buzzing sound, yet it wasn't even switched on! *Well, that figures!* With a sigh, he switched the computer on and waited. When it had powered up and the OS had loaded, he logged in and typed *monkey* into Google. Almost 700 million hits. *Gold monkey* returned only 400,000 or so. He switched to looking at images instead. He scrolled through the pictures until one caught his eye. It was a picture of Sun Wukong, the Monkey King. Bingo!

Sanjeev zoomed in on the picture until it filled the screen. It showed Sun Wukong standing on top of a cloud, a great red cape billowing out behind him. A bright yellow robe covered all of his golden fur but for his hands and face. A gold headband circled his head. Sun Wukong had bared his teeth, which made him look like he was laughing. He held a long staff at his side, its ends capped with gold.

He looked at the gold key again. Sanjeev did another quick search and pulled up some more information on the Monkey King. The Monkey King story was apparently one of the most popular of all Chinese legends – and here he was hearing it for the first time! Sanjeev was hooked right from the start. As soon as he read that Monkey was born inside a magic stone, he knew it was going to be excellent.

It seemed Monkey was always getting in trouble, not just with other monkeys but also with the Jade Emperor, the monarch of all the gods in Heaven. In search for a weapon, Monkey visited the dragon king of the Eastern Seas who told him he could have a giant, eight-tonne staff – if he could lift it from the ocean floor. The staff glowed as he approached, signifying the presence of its true master. Lifting it with ease, Sun Wukong found that it had magic powers as well – it could change size, multiply, even fight on its own if his master wished. Monkey made it shrink to the size of a needle and kept it behind his ear. In addition to the staff, Sun Wukong acquired other magic weapons: a golden mail shirt, a cap with phoenix feathers, and cloud-walking boots.

Eventually, Sun Wukong became so powerful he decided to take on Heaven. He learned the seventy-two Earthly Transformations – how to change shape into all kinds of animals and objects. Already a mighty, immensely strong warrior, he also learned spells to freeze humans and gods, spells to command wind and water, and how to make protective circles.

When Monkey got to the mythical Jade Palace, the Jade Emperor decided it was better not to fight him, and better to hire him! That didn't work out too well. Sun Wukong got into the Heavenly Peach Garden, ate the peaches of immortality, consumed Pills of Immortality and drank the Jade Emperor's wine.

Enough was enough, said the Jade Emperor, and he and the gods tried to take Monkey down, but Sun Wukong single-handedly defeated ten thousand celestial warriors in battle. Things got so bad they had to call in Buddha, the wisest of all.

Buddha made Sun Wukong a bet: Sun Wukong would be free to go if he could escape from Buddha's palm. Sun Wukong accepted and flew all the way to the end of the world where he found five great pillars. He marked them to show he had escaped, only to find they were Buddha's fingers. Monkey jumped back into Buddha's palm. To stop Monkey from escaping, Buddha turned his hand into a mountain and buried Sun Wukong under it, where he remained trapped for the next 500 years.

'Wow!' Sanjeev gasped. 'Sun Wukong was totally epic, in every sense of the word.'

Sanjeev scrolled back up to the top of the page to read more about where the story came from. Sun Wukong was over a thousand years old, from the Song Dynasty. His stories were part of a larger tale – *The Journey to the West*, written in the 16th century by Wu Cheng'en about the travels of a monk named Tang Xuanzang who goes on a pilgrimage in search of holy texts. Sun Wukong, along with other Immortals exiled to the human world, joined the monk to protect him.

It was all fascinating stuff. But it still didn't answer one of the biggest of the many, *many* big questions rattling around his brain: why had they given the key to him? And was the key really as solid and real as he thought it was?

CHAPTER 46

—

Pushing back his chair, Sanjeev stood up. The buzzing sound coming from his computer hadn't gone away and was really bugging him. What could it be? Was his computer about to die? Stepping away from the desk, he went back to his bed and picked up the silvery slice. *I should put this away before anyone sees it*, he was thinking when Jigsaw, who had been sitting quietly while Sanjeev surfed the net, suddenly decided he needed to have more attention.

Before Sanjeev could stop him, Jigsaw rose up and smacked his front paws on Sanjeev's chest. Knocked off balance, Sanjeev staggered backwards towards the desk, the silvery slice still in his hand. As soon as he did so, the buzzing sound doubled in volume, its penetrating metallic thrum filling the air and hurting Sanjeev's ears.

With Jigsaw's paws still on his chest, Sanjeev forced the dog to hop backwards as they both moved away from the desk and the computer. As they moved away, the buzzing sound lessened until it was the same level as before. Jigsaw put all four legs on the ground and Sanjeev frowned. As Jigsaw stood wagging his tail, Sanjeev took a step towards the computer with the silvery slice in his hand. The horrible noise increased once more.

'Hmmm,' Sanjeev said. He took another step. And another. And another. Each time the noise got louder and louder. Then, one finger in his ear and holding the slice in his other hand, he leaned as close as he dared towards the computer, closing his eyes tightly and waiting for what might happen next...

He opened his eyes. The strange buzzing sound had stopped and a message had appeared on the dark screen. To be precise, it was a dialogue between someone called First Hare and someone called Second Hare. The cursor, Sanjeev noticed, was blinking on the line that said, *Second Hare*.

THE THREE HARES

First Hare: Hello?
Second Hare: |

Sanjeev reached forward, punched in some letters, and hit enter. Almost immediately, his words appeared next to Second Hare. Sanjeev's heart thumped in his chest.

The First Hare's reply was instantaneous.

THE THREE HARES

Second Hare: Hello?

First Hare: Finally!

Second Hare: Finally? What do you mean, finally?

First Hare: I mean finally someone answered me.

Second Hare: Hold on. Let me get this straight. You've been waiting ages for someone you didn't know to answer you?

First Hare: Months and months!

Second Hare: And why did you post the message?

First Hare: It's a long story.

Second Hare: Okay. What's your name?

First Hare: You can call me the First Hare. And I've no idea how the discussion group 'The Three Hares' got started. It just appeared on my screen.

Second Hare: Mine too. So where are you from?

First Hare: China. You?

Second Hare: NJ.

First Hare: NJ?

Second Hare: New Jersey, USA.

First Hare: I know where New Jersey is.

Second Hare: So why'd you ask what NJ was?

First Hare: Could have been New Junction!

Second Hare: New Junction? Where's that?

First Hare: England.

Second Hare: How do you know that?

First Hare: I just do.

Second Hare: Did you Google it?

First Hare: Maybe.

Second Hare: So are you Chinese?

First Hare: My mother is.

Second Hare: I was wondering because your English is really good.

First Hare: Pfff. Thank you so much, I guess. BTW you haven't told me who you are.

Second Hare: And you haven't told me who you are!

First Hare: That's because I'm not going to.

Second Hare: You sound suspicious.

First Hare: I am.

Second Hare: Why?

First Hare: I know a couple of brothers at my school who like playing stupid pranks.

Second Hare: Three brothers?

First Hare: No – just two of them. Who are the three brothers?

Second Hare: Doesn't matter. What about the brothers at your school? What's this got to do with them?

First Hare: I need to know you aren't one of them. I need to know you aren't playing a trick.

Second Hare: Okay. How can I prove that I'm for real?

First Hare: Have you ever heard of Bai Lu?

Second Hare: Nope. What's that? Oh, wait! Something kind of weird happened to me at the airport when I was saying goodbye to my uncle.

First Hare: Weird like what?

Second Hare: Nothing, probably. It was that my uncle was talking about that company – Bai Lu – and then... Well, I dunno exactly what happened. I was somewhere else, sort of floating.

Sanjeev waited.

Second Hare: Hello? You still there? Hello? Hello?

First Hare: Hi. Did you see something – a boy with black eyes?

Second Hare: Yeah. How did you know?

First Hare: The same thing happened to me.

There was another pause before the First Hare continued again.

First Hare: If I asked you to describe something silver and about the size of a slice of pizza, would you know what I was talking about?

Second Hare: One word: hare!

First Hare: :-) Okay, Good.

Second Hare: Good?

First Hare: Good! I believe you.

Second Hare: It's always good to be believed! :-) Thought I was going to have to carry my crazy story to the grave – that I'd be put away if I told anyone.

First Hare: We've got an awful lot to talk about – starting with the triskelion.

Second Hare: The what?

First Hare: It's an ancient symbol. I'm pasting in from Wikipedia.

Second Hare: So how did you get yours?

First Hare: First, tell me how you got yours.

Sanjeev paused, stretched his fingers, and began.

CHAPTER 47

—

It was after midnight when Sanjeev switched off his computer. He listened. Downstairs, his father was locking the back door to the garden. The pitter-pattering of Jigsaw's claws as he trotted across the kitchen floor towards his basket followed, then, 'Good night, boy.' Sanjeev dashed across the room to his bed. His mother had already told him to log off, and that had been an hour ago. He threw back the quilt, jumped in, switched off his bedside light, and pulled the quilt up to his chin – just in time. His bedroom door creaked open and a shaft of light fell into the room.

'Go to sleep,' his father said.

Sanjeev said nothing.

'I know you're not sleeping because you aren't snoring!'

'Good night, Dad.'

'Night, son,' his father said and was about to close the door when he spoke again. 'Oh by the way, your mother left a message about the woman who helped you find Jigsaw. On the way home, I saw her outside the station…'

Sanjeev propped himself up on his elbows.

'I know a guy who runs a shelter. We got her a place to stay tonight.'

Sanjeev nodded. 'That's great, Dad. Thanks.'

His father smiled. 'Now go to sleep.'

Instead, Sanjeev sneezed loudly.

His mother came in. 'Still not asleep!' she said and immediately placed a hand on his forehead. 'Hmmm… no temperature.'

'I'm fine,' Sanjeev said, leaning away. 'Actually, I'm glad you're both here. There's something I forgot to tell you.' His mother and father looked at one another, then back at him.

'Well? What is it?' his mother asked.

'I think I've made up my mind. I'm going to become a veterinarian.'

'Really? Why?'

'Well,' Sanjeev said, taking a moment to put his thoughts into words. For one thing, it *felt* right. 'I realised how much animals depend on us when we take them out of the wild. That they need us as much as we need them.'

His mother smiled. 'Oh! That's great! I think you'll love being surrounded by animals and helping them get better. We are very proud of you, Sanjeev,' his mother said. She kissed him on the forehead and tucked him in.

Sanjeev lay back down. He wanted to sleep, but after the *monumental* day he had had, drifting off was impossible. Lying in darkness and staring up at the ceiling, he thought of the conversation with the First Hare – whose name, he had discovered, was Sara. What a day!

After Sanjeev had told Sara everything that had happened in the Met – the mosaic, the travelling back in time, meeting the Immortals, the gold key and silvery slice he had brought back – Sara had decided she could trust him. Her story – about how she had to take a Jade Dragonball to some princess and was given a piece of silk – sounded as crazy as his: they had both met at least some of the Immortals, and they had both brought back two objects each that no one else but they could see. What really puzzled them was why.

Why had they been chosen? Why were they given the objects? Why did the Immortals need *them*?

During the conversation, Sara had mentioned that she travelled to the UK every year to see her grandmother. And that had given Sanjeev an idea. Sanjeev's father was looking forward to watching cricket in the summer with Uncle Manoj in London, where they usually stopped for a few days before travelling to India to see their other relatives.

'Why don't we meet while we're in London?' he had suggested.

'Where?' Sara had asked.

Sanjeev had thought about it. It had to be somewhere that was easy to get to. It also had to be somewhere their families would be happy to take them.

'How about the British Museum?' Sara had suggested. 'My grandmother lives close to it.'

Perfect. So that was the plan. They would keep in touch and try to meet in London next summer.

After that, Sara had told him about the research she had done on the Three Hares and the Silk Road, and Sanjeev had asked her about the Eight Immortals. He'd never even heard of them before today, but Sara had. They were an important part of Chinese culture, according to her. It wasn't something that Sanjeev knew much about.

Sanjeev closed his eyes. The biggest unknown was the reason why. It all seemed so... random. And yet, there *were* similarities in Sara's and his experiences. They were able to communicate on a discussion forum that had popped out of nowhere. They were both, it seemed, able to travel in time. They had been congratulated at the end of their adventures as though they had passed a test. Was all of this evidence of some grand plan? Of powers operating beyond the known laws of the universe? Were the Immortals responsible? If they were and if there was a purpose to their actions, they hadn't disclosed it, or he and Sara hadn't discovered it. Yet.

Sanjeev sighed. So many questions; so many things to think about.

One thing was for sure: he couldn't wait for summer to arrive – but something made him feel wary, too.

With a vague sense of foreboding, it was late into the night before he finally drifted to sleep. And as he slipped into his dreams, one more thought whispered to him, stirring his mind gently like a breeze trembling leaves: *The third hare. Who is the third hare?*

PART 8

XI'AN — THE
PRESENT DAY

Chapter 48

━

After journeying through the storm, Chan, An Ho and Yang had landed in a remote airfield in rural Pennsylvania and climbed into a waiting jet. Then they had made two refuelling stops: one in a tiny airstrip on the west coast of America near Mount Washington Wilderness, and the other in a country where a certain amount of money had ensured that the customs officers who boarded the jet checked their passports and not the large, wooden crate in the cargo hold.

Flying out of that country, Chan had breathed more easily. It was the last leg of their epic journey and their precious cargo was safely stowed. But even in the most luxurious private jet that money could buy, Chan was unable to close his eyes for more than a few seconds at a time.

When the Bai Lu pilot finally announced they were entering Chinese airspace, time slowed down for Chan. His dreams were so close, every second of delay felt like an eternity. Their destination was Xi'an Xianyang International Airport, the closest airport to Xi'an and the factory where Project Tian Shan was currently underway, and where it would be soon complete. At last, he had collected all the pieces of the jigsaw: Lin Dan, the jade suit, and, of course, the Jade Dragonball.

A Bai Lu company helicopter was waiting for them when their jet landed. Chan watched nervously as the crate was unloaded from the jet and transferred to the helicopter for the journey to Xi'an.

At the same time, Zhou Shi arrived with the Jade Dragonball, as instructed. Bowing deeply, he presented it to Chan. Soon they were all flying towards the city, with Mount Huashan – one of the most famous mountains in China – in the distance. For thousands of years, it had dominated the area, guarding the central plains, the Yellow River and the Wei River. On its ridges, the first emperor had built the Great Wall of China – under the stones of which thousands of workers had been buried.

But thoughts of how many had died making the Great Wall was not what was keeping Chan awake. Instead, it was the importance of the box they carried. As they had left American airspace, it had begun to make itself felt, an invisible force enveloping Chan's body and pressing it from all sides. As soon as they entered Chinese airspace, the force had increased, its amplified pulsing making every bone in Chan's body vibrate as though he were a string being plucked. It was as if the suit knew it was home.

And as the pulsing increased, so did Chan's excitement. It grew stronger with every metre they progressed. He gave a mirthless laugh. *Nothing can stop me now.* 'They thought I was a fool,' he said to no one in particular. 'But they were wrong and now I have the Dragonball and the jade suit.'

Cong, the helicopter pilot, was unaccustomed to being spoken to. 'Sir?' he said, speaking into the mic attached to his headphones. When Chan did not respond, Cong continued. 'Boss, if you will pardon my question, what's so special about the Dragonball?'

Chan ignored the question. Smiling ruefully, he said instead, 'My father amassed great wealth while an even greater treasure lay submerged, just out of reach. But now I have it.' He reached over and stroked the Jade Dragonball, which was sitting in a box beside him. 'The places I have been in search of you!' he murmured.

And it was true. He had travelled from the frozen wastes of the Heilongjian province in the north to the mountains of Guilin that rose like stalagmites in the region of Guangxi in the south. In each of these places, and countless more, he had consulted the most renowned fortune tellers alive. He remembered Kumamoto, at the southern tip of Japan. There he had found Nosuke Hiro, a practitioner of Syō-Kan – the Four Pillars of Destiny – who had tried to tell him his destiny and had spouted some nonsense about a silk scarf that was some kind of knife. *Fool! Liar and fraud!*

In retrospect, it was clear that Pythias had truly been a master. Now, the meaning of all but one vision he had seen while visiting Pythias had been solved. The fish had swallowed the Dragonball and was no longer a puzzle. But what of the rabbits? What did they mean?

Chan paused. Zhou Shi had also brought him the gold box in which he kept the mooncake he so loved. He gave Zhou Shi a nod of approval. Clearly the man was useful. 'Has our guest been brought to Xi'an?' Chan asked.

'Yes, boss. He is waiting there. Everything is arranged.'

Chan nodded. Turning away, he chewed on the slice of the cake. A vision of the burning hwamei rose in front of his eyes. 'The Greek,' he whispered. Did he feel sorry about having Pythias killed? Hardly! But he did regret it: without the old man, he might not discover the meaning of the rabbits easily. But he had come this far. The road had been difficult, but he had persevered. The meaning, he felt certain, would not escape him forever…

Cong had waited respectfully while Chan lost himself in his thoughts. He flipped off the wipers. The snow had lessened so that only the odd flake was falling, as if in slow motion. 'Boss,' he said, 'may I ask you a question?'

Chan nodded wearily.

'What's the big thing for?' Cong asked. 'The thing in the crate.'

Chan smiled. The Jade Dragonball was partially hidden in the box's purple cloth. Chan took the Jade Dragonball out and hefted it in his hand. It felt heavy. He imagined the soul trapped within, and wondered how much it weighed. The seaweed that clung to it had long ago been carefully scraped off so that now its highly polished exterior revealed the intricacy of the carvings: dragons so life-like it seemed they would soon wriggle free. Chan smiled and held the Dragonball up. 'It's for him.'

CHAPTER 49

An hour and a half later, they arrived in Xi'an. Driving slowly along a back alley in a quiet suburb of the city, the limo and truck drew to a halt while two rickety, red doors behind some shops and a cheap cafe were swung open. The limo slowly crossed the threshold, followed by the truck. Both crawled into a long wooden barn – their rumbling arrival disturbing a family of birds roosting in the rafters. The limo and truck cut their engines. The door to the barn was slammed shut, a button was pressed, and slowly the limo and truck began sinking into the ground, lowered by a massive hydraulic lift.

When the machinery hissed and stopped, the limo and truck were in a tunnel that stretched away on either side. Bare strip lights, spaced at broad intervals, ran the length of the tunnel's ceiling, casting a chalky light. All was silent. Then, with a roar, the limo and truck restarted their engines and trundled forward.

Fifteen minutes later, the tunnel opened into a well-lit atrium. The limo came to a halt and its driver – An Ho – got out to open Chan's door. Chan stepped out, followed by Yang and Zhou Shi, and stood in front of the men who were waiting expectantly. The truck parked and Yang called over a couple of other men. Together they retrieved the crate from inside.

Once the crate had been removed, Chan held up the Jade Dragonball. All of the men bowed deeply.

'Our greatest success,' Chan said, the cave amplifying his words so that they sounded as if they had been spoken by a giant, 'is close. Soon, the words Bai Lu shall be on everyone's lips.'

The men cheered and Chan led the way, with An Ho, Yang and Zhou Shi a few steps behind him. Off to the left, the tunnels led to the dining halls, the sleeping quarters and lab. To the right, a large waterfall flowed, driving a torrent of water through the underground hideaway.

They entered a circular room lit by torches set in sconces on the walls. Hanging in an alcove was a scroll with calligraphy done in the grass style, using lines so wavy and connected they bore little resemblance to common Chinese characters. Filling the opposite wall was an ink painting of two cranes standing below ripe peaches that hung from a branch above their heads, peonies blooming at their feet. On a third wall was a multi-coloured mandala – a set of nested squares inside a larger circle. The fourth wall held an elegant painting that depicted imperial life – the original, priceless *Spring Morning in the Han Palace,* a handscroll by Qiu Ying.

Chan went to a low table and picked up a wooden spoon that lay on its side next to a large brass bowl, which was sitting on a red pillow with golden tassels at each corner. Half the wooden spoon's length was covered in black silk, richly embroidered with interlocking circles in golden thread. Reaching down, Chan ran the end of the spoon not covered in silk round and round the inner rim of the bowl, until it emitted the ghost of a hum. He smiled, listening as An Ho, Yang and Zhou Shi brought in the crate containing the jade suit and set it down beside a great, golden dais. An Ho retrieved a long crowbar. He placed the end between the slats in the crate and carefully pried apart the wood while Zhou Shi and Yang held the crate in place. The snapping wood echoed loudly in the chamber.

'Gently, An Ho. We have not come this far to have you smash it to bits,' Chan said. 'They believe this stolen,' he said, pointing at the crate, 'but I have only reclaimed what was ours.'

An Ho removed the cover of the crate to reveal the jade suit – thousands of small pieces of jade strung together with gold wire to make a torso, arms, legs. Chan could hardly breathe: the suit was so beautiful. The three of them reached into the crate, and together moved the suit onto the dais. Carefully, An Ho and Zhou Shi folded the suit's hands together, resting them on the suit's lower torso. Now the hands were ready to receive what Chan had searched so long to possess.

Chan laid his hand upon the suit, felt its cold stone. 'Fragments of the Jade Palace, home of the Immortals. It did not sustain its previous owner, the wife of Prince Liu Yingke, nephew of Emperor Liu Bang, founder of the Han Dynasty. But of course, she did not know what was required.'

With a nod from Chan, Jang stepped behind Zhou Shi and drew a blade across Zhou's throat. Zhou Shi's arms and legs twitched and then fell still.

'Under his chin. Catch it all,' Chan told An Ho, handing him a bowl. An Ho placed the bowl to Zhou's chest. The blood ran down Zhou Shi's chest like a red river. When the bowl was full, Jang loosened his grip on the body. It fell limply to the floor.

Chan felt all the years of searching fall behind him, felt himself borne up by the momentum Project Tian Shan was gathering. Zhou Shi had been a smart boy – sharp, attentive. But most importantly, he had come from a long line of *fangshi* – occult masters. It was the blood of such magicians, alchemists, necromancers and mystics – the boy's ancestors – that had to be spilled.

The suit demanded a fangshi blood sacrifice.

Years of searching had led Chan down paths toward a bewildering array of sacred bits of knowledge, spread out across the stacks of book, scrolls, and parchments in his enormous library. Enough for him to piece together at least some of the steps to follow in a most secretive ritual. 'To neither the 33 realms of Heaven…' Chan cried. Taking the golden bowl from An Ho in one hand and the Jade Dragonball in the other, he raised both above the jade suit, 'nor the 153 jails of Hell shall I go!' His reedy voice grew stronger. 'Suit! I command thee to serve! I command thee to bring him forth! I command thee to be the eternal saviour, defeating all that ages and diminishes!' And with those words, he tipped the contents of the bowl onto the suit, allowing a steady trickle to trace a weaving path over the jade fragments, head to toe. His eyes as fiery as the torches around him, he cradled the Jade Dragonball in his palm above his head.

As he watched, a faint, yellow light deep within the suit ignited, at first no brighter than a single candle. But astonishingly quickly, it grew in intensity, until, as bright as the sun, it burst forth, a searing light pulsing from every centimetre of jade.

Shielding his eyes, Chan dropped the bowl of blood and clung with both hands to the Jade Dragonball, which he still held aloft and which was vibrating and humming like a million angry bees were trapped within. The noise rose and rose, shaking Chan's whole body, filling the tiny room with pulses of sound so loud they pushed against the men like crashing sea waves.

'I can't…' Chan cried, his knees buckling. 'Help…' But Jang and An Ho, pressed hard against the wall themselves, could not do anything. Leaning towards their boss, the skin on their faces rippling back as though they were fighting against a hurricane, they barely managed to lift a hand. The men fell to their knees.

Suddenly, a volcano of tiny particles spewed from the top of the Dragonball, rising into the air, striking the ceiling, pouring down the walls, scuttling across the ground, and climbing the thighs and chests of Chan, An Ho and Jang.

Chan opened his mouth, tried to scream: the particles were a scorching, scalding agony. But he could not draw a breath. The emptied Jade Dragonball tumbled from his hands and he fell forward, landing face first on the dirt floor, the suit on the table above him.

The suit glowed red, orange, yellow, and white. Just as the suit and life itself began to recede from Chan, the particles sprang away as if they were iron filaments being drawn by a savagely powerful magnet. Chan raised his eyes.

The particles were assembling themselves in front of his nose: a toe, a foot, an ankle, a shin...

Chan drew a desperately needed breath.

... two legs, a stomach, a torso, a chest...

Chan raised his chest from the ground and glanced at An Ho, who, eyes wide, was staring at the fiery body, the glowing, amber-coloured living sculpture forming.

... shoulders, a neck, a head...

Panting, Chan tucked his legs below himself. The face composed of a billion flickering sparks looked regally down at him. Chan gasped and bowed deeply, so deep his forehead touched the dirt.

The Master had arrived.

CHAPTER 50

As he continued to bow, the damp smell of packed earth rose into Chan's nose. How he had waited for this moment, how he had dreamed of—

'You fool! You idiotic blunderer! I am still too weak!'

Chan's head snapped up. His eyes met the Master's. Chan opened his mouth, but before he could say a word, the Master turned, and laying a knee on the table, he hoisted himself onto it.

'But…' Chan said, standing and drawing nearer the table. Where the Master had touched the tabletop, particles like hot honey had spread themselves but quickly rejoined the Master's body. The Master reached one hand across the jade suit and, as though he were taking a hot bath, he lowered himself into the suit.

The particles, fizzing and leaping, slipped through the suit's gold wires until all were contained within the suit's confines. Below the pieces of jade, the particles seethed, tiny spumes rising and falling like magma in a chamber.

Chan, dazed and astonished by the Master's rebuke, turned at the sound of An Ho's padded footsteps as he approached. His eyes fell unfocused on An Ho's face. It made little sense. Why had the Master been angry? He, Chan, had brought him the jade suit. He, Chan, had released him from the Jade Dragonball. Why—

'Boss!'

Chan, refocusing, followed An Ho's pointed finger.

His eyes locked on the suit. There, like the glowing embers of a furnace, a circular, red-orange pattern had formed – one Chan knew immediately. His mind reeled back to Pythias, to the visions he had seen while in the oracle's filthy apartment.

Chan staggered back and almost fell.

'The triskelion, you fool!' Shan Wu's harsh whisper reverberated in the room. How had he, Chan, been so stupid? Without the Three Hares triskelion, the Master's reanimation could not be complete. He would have to shelter in the confines of the jade suit, suspended somewhere between this world and the one beyond. The Master had known that! He had known all along he needed the triskelion!

Breathing hard, Chan struggled to master his emotions. Now that he too understood what he had seen in Athens, it was infuriatingly, ridiculously obvious. As the outline of the triskelion blazed upon the jade suit, he recalled all he knew of the triskelion's meaning. Most fangshi said it was a strange loop, a motif representing abundance, fertility and peace.

However, a few renegade fangshi of The White Ink school disagreed. Their books had been burned, ignored and ridiculed. They had been called madmen. And what, according to these fangshi, was the triskelion's true meaning? Simply put, it was *to be*. According to these White Ink scholars, the ancients had searched for a way to represent matter arising from energy, fullness from emptiness, and ultimately the universe from nothing.

Chan licked his dry lips. The Three Hares triskelion, if The White Ink school was correct, bestowed upon its possessor the powers of a divine creator.

While Chan, Jang and An Ho watched, the burning red imprint of the triskelion on the jade suit's chest began to fade. Then, as though water had been poured on the suit and was dousing its flames, the suit's inner glow also began to diminish, the red growing paler and paler until it was gone entirely and the suit was returned to a patchwork collection of jade squares, illuminated by flickering torchlight but nothing else.

Chan leaned forward and peered inside. The dancing, writhing particles had gone and in their place was a pale, withered body, its desiccated face taut, its eyes tightly shut, its skeletal arms and legs as thin as dried twigs.

He looked like a body that had been buried in the hot sands of the Taklamakan Desert for a thousand years. And yet, the Master was breathing.

When at last Chan spoke, his voice was unnaturally calm. 'Take the bowl,' he said, picking it up and handing it to Jang, 'and take that away.' Chan told An Ho, nodding to the body of Zhou Shi.

'Yes, boss,' An Ho replied, and grabbed Zhou Shi by the scruff of the neck. Zhou Shi's legs made a scuffling sound as they trailed away. 'Anything else, boss?' An Ho asked, he and Jang waiting at the door.

Chan paused, forcing himself to swallow his disappointment and think of what he should do next. As his eyes drifted over the jade suit and he pondered how the failure to bring Shan Wu fully back to life might affect Project Tian Shan, an idea struck him. 'Yes... Once you have finished, An Ho, you can accompany me to the guest quarters.'

An Ho's face was blank and his mind, too: one of his men whose thoughts were inaccessible to him. Some minds were. Chan assumed it was the emptiness of their heads! No matter. An Ho did whatever was asked of him. And, of course, he never asked questions.

'Yes, boss,' An Ho replied.

'And Jang?'

'Yes, boss?'

'Come back when you're done and clean up,' Chan said, noting with distaste the long, red streak following Zhou Shi's body like an unfurling tail.

CHAPTER 51

When Chan entered Lin Dan's cell, Lin Dan turned away from his computer and faced him, but not before he had hit the screen lock – hiding the model of a stretch of DNA where a gene was producing an interesting protein. Chan willed his face to remain impassive. *Did he really imagine his actions could be hidden from me?*

The computer Lin Dan was working on was not, of course, connected to the internet. However, it did have a massive library of technical journals downloaded to its hard drive along with all the programs Lin Dan could ever want. It also had spyware that provided Chan with a mirror screen showing him everything Lin Dan did, recording every complex calculation Lin Dan made. That, along with the dozen micro-cameras inside the cell meant Chan could follow Lin Dan's every move.

Chan, followed by An Ho, came to the table where Lin Dan was working. Lin Dan, he thought, looked tired: his eyes were red and sagged from lack of sleep; his skin was grey; his clothes – though he had been provided with fresh ones – were the same as he had worn in Shanghai. It was clear captivity didn't agree with him.

What Lin Dan needed, Chan decided, was something to cheer him up. Perhaps his favourite meal? Or a call to his family? Or both. Yes, he decided, let him have both: he needed this man to be as happy and motivated as circumstances allowed. Admittedly, this cell was now his permanent home until the completion of Project Tian Shan. But as Sun Tzu said: 'Treat your men as you would your own beloved sons and they will follow you into the deepest valley.'

'I trust you are enjoying our hospitality,' Chan said

As soon as he said it, Lin Dan clenched his jaw. Perhaps to him it seemed like an eternity since he had been blindfolded, put on a plane, and brought here. In reality, it had only been a few days. Nevertheless, Chan was sure Lin Dan had come to hate him more than any other man he had ever known. When Lin Dan did not speak, Chan continued. 'Perhaps you have made some progress?' Chan asked. He glanced at An Ho, who stood on the other side of the table, as solid and immobile as a statue.

Lin Dan loosened his jaw and cleared his throat. 'Fingerite is not only rare, it is also difficult to work with. If I were back at my lab…'

'I am afraid that is not possible,' Chan said, his voice flat. He gestured at the food tray on the desk, the mound of rice and vegetables untouched. 'But perhaps your work would improve if you ate? Does our cuisine displease you?'

'No, no, it is good,' Lin Dan said.

Chan could tell he was lying. 'Let my staff know what meal you would like and they shall see to it.'

After a pause, Lin Dan said: 'Thank you.' The tone was empty of gratitude.

'I have also arranged, once again, for you to call your family. They will enjoy hearing more details about your new job here. Let them share in the excitement—'

'If you harm them in any way, I'll—' Lin Dan cried, eyes blazing, jumping to his feet.

'I've already assured you I will not… as long as you keep your side of the bargain.' He held Lin Dan's stare, aware of An Ho twitching forward. He gave a shake of the head and An Ho backed away.

Lin Dan, towering over Chan, brushed away a clump of the shaggy hair that covered his eyes and reminded Chan of a shih-tzu. 'I said I will, so I will.' Lin Dan's voice was almost a whisper.

'I didn't tell you the good news, did I?' Chan said cheerily.

Lin Dan eyed him suspiciously.

Chan continued. 'I suppose you know Northgate International school…'

Lin Dan did not reply, but Chan knew he had piqued Lin Dan's interest. Northgate was one of the premier and most exclusive educational institutions in Shanghai. Even if parents could afford the astronomical fees, the children still had to pass interviews and exams to gain acceptance. Chan smiled. 'Even for their preschool classes, they have, as I am sure you already know, a very long waiting list. But I am very pleased to tell you they have accepted Yuqi.'

A rush of thoughts from Lin Dan flooded Chan's mind. 'I should also give you this,' Chan said, and reaching over, he placed a piece of paper he had taken from his pocket on Lin Dan's hand. Lin Dan scanned the printed paper – his bank, his account – and his eyes widened. 'We like to take care of our best employees,' Chan said. 'That is a… signing on bonus. I hope you will accept it.'

Chan was about to tell Lin Dan to sit, but before he could, Lin Dan's legs seemed to go weak and he flopped onto the chair.

Chan drew a little closer. 'You know, it will be an honour for you,' Chan said, 'to have played a part in a project of such historic importance – when it comes to fruition.'

Lin Dan frowned. 'You have not fully explained—'

'Ah, but I will,' Chan cut in. 'I assure you. And when the project succeeds, your name will appear in science textbooks across the world for years to come.'

'But I can't—' Lin Dan started again. 'I'm not free to leave, am I?'

'Calamity has its roots in prosperity; prosperity its roots in calamity,' Chan said softly and paused, letting the words of proverb linger in the air; then: 'The circumstances are difficult. I acknowledge this. But there is an opportunity here to do great things.'

Lin Dan hung his head.

'I have a question,' Chan announced.

Lin Dan reluctantly returned his eyes to Chan's face.

'Have you ever taken a DNA sample from a 1,000-year-old subject?'

Lin Dan slowly shook his head and inwardly Chan smiled: a spark of interest had brightened Lin Dan's eyes. 'No, never,' the scientist replied.

'Well,' Chan said, allowing the smile to transfer to his lips, 'I think it's time we rectified that.'

PART 9

THE JADE PALACE ⊢
THE PRESENT DAY

CHAPTER 52

Wispy clouds as soft as baby hair drifted over Zhang Guolao's bare feet and knees. Sitting crossed-legged, hands lightly clasped, chin up, he was in one of his favourite places: the Jade Palace's central courtyard beside the Fountain of Eternal Life, whose precious waters were burbling and tinkling pleasantly in his ears.

Though Zhang Guolao's eyes were closed, he was not asleep. Instead, he was meditating, which meant that as he slowly emptied his lungs, he was concentrating hard on every molecule of air flowing from his slightly parted mouth. He was not a true master of meditation, others were far more accomplished; nevertheless, he liked to spend at least an hour a day away from the others, in peace, alone with his thoughts, at one with the universe... a long-legged fly upon the stream of time. Zhang Guolao smiled at the image. Nature was a limitless source of nourish—

'You are *such* a child, Lan Caihe. Why don't you grow up?' He heard Xiangu's scolding voice.

'Listen to Little Miss Perfect! Go and waft your lotus blossom somewhere else and leave me alone, okay?'

'Enough! I can't hear myself think,' Zhongli Quan growled.

'Where's my sword? Who's been mucking about with my...Oh, there it is.' Lu Dongbin, sounding sheepish.

Zhang Guolao sighed. That was the problem living with seven other Immortals: one had to listen to them all day, every day, for the rest of time. Wearying, to say the least. A loosened strand of

Zhang Guolao's grey hair tickled his cheek. He took a long, deep breath, feeling his diaphragm expand as he sucked in air. The others wandered past him and out of the courtyard, their voices beginning to recede.

He returned his full attention to his breathing and smiled contentedly. A long-legged fly upon the stream of time. Yes; yes, indeed. An image of still water in a pool dappled with sunlight entered his mind. A summer breeze rose and the water rippled. The ripples multiplied, lapping at the pool's edges. The pool grew larger, its water overflowing its shallow banks, tricking in all directions. The sun slipped behind clouds. The air grew heavier, chillier. The pool became a lake. Waves coursed across its water and crashed on its shores. And then the vision was upon Zhang Guolao, immersing him in its thrashing, dark world.

'No!' Zhang Guolao cried, trying to open his eyes, leave what he was being shown. But he could not. The vision was not done with him. And as Zhang Guolao moaned and struggled, it continued, locking its arms around him, clutching him to its world like a body might its skin until finally, *finally*, it was over and Zhang Guolao, panting, shaking, was released.

Zhang Guolao's trembling hands wiped away the strands of hair and the tears from his cheeks. They, the Eight Immortals, had enlisted the help of the Three Hares for one purpose only: to prevent a drop of the Elixir of Immortality from touching a single human's lips. The reason was simple. Humans were incapable of handling the responsibility. They were weak. They were immature. They demanded their lives had meaning, searched for it high and low. And when their end drew near, they told themselves they'd lived a good life, or not. Because that was what death was: a sentence with a full stop. Nothing else made it complete; nothing else gave life its meaning but death.

And anyway, the *Eight* were the Immortals; no one else; certainly not the whole of humanity. Did they deserve to have and keep the love and reverence humans gave them? Perhaps; perhaps not. But this vision of the future, this... impending horror? The Three Hares were no longer just soldiers protecting the Eight. They were protecting the whole of humanity.

Unsteadily, Zhang Guolao rose to his feet and stumbling but gathering pace, he called to the others who, backs turned, were entering a doorway of the palace.

'A vision! A vision!' he yelled, the words echoing from the Jade Palace's towering walls. Heads swivelled and mouths opened. For a moment, they did nothing. But then all at once, they came running, quickly catching him up.

'What did you see?' Lan Caihe cried, his boyish face creased.

Zhang Guolao, chest heaving, waved his question away and continued across the courtyard.

'Was it bad?' Lan Caihe persisted. 'Tell us!'

Zhang Guolao had had these visions of the future before. None had been good. No longer running but walking as fast as he could, he entered a long corridor that seemed to be suspended and unsupported in the sky, and nodded curtly. Occasional white fluffy clouds wafted around them as he walked, shimmering in the sunlight.

The others, striding by his side, were as silent and grim-faced as Zhang Guolao until: 'Watch out!' Zhongli Quan said, pointing.

Zhang Guolao peered along the corridor's mirrored walls to the objects in the distance. On a jade pedestal twice the size of a house, a page on the Book of Immutable Deeds was curling, getting ready to fall. They braced themselves. The page fell and a torrent of air rushed at and past them, pushing at their bodies and ruffling their robes and hair.

'Hurry!' Zhang Guolao said, and ignoring the pain in his leg making him limp, he led them closer and closer to the Book until at last they were next to it.

Together, they stared mutely at the Book and the tiny, ant-like words being written vertically on its freshly-turned page by an unseen hand. Zhongli Quan felt the blood in his face draining. The others looked as shocked. The words in the Book of Immutable Deeds, the eternal chronicle of human fate, action and inaction, continued to tumble down the parchment, telling of a great darkness that threatened, of untold misery, of millions afflicted, the pain and suffering on a scale beyond all reckoning, every word, every terrifying detail adding to the horror. And then the words stopped. The Eight looked at one another, too aghast to speak. Now the words – such horrifying, loathsome words! – had been written in the Book, the future had been sealed. One power, only if concentrated in the right hands, could make it otherwise.